COTTAGE HOSPITAL

COTTAGE HOSPITAL

Claire Rayner

This revised edition, complete with new introduction,
first published in Great Britain 1993 by
SEVERN HOUSE PUBLISHERS LTD of
9–15 High Street, Sutton, Surrey SM1 1DF.
Originally published 1963 in paperback format only by
Transworld Publishers Ltd under the pseudonym of Sheila Brandon.
First published in the U.S.A. 1993 by
SEVERN HOUSE PUBLISHERS INC., of
475 Fifth Avenue, New York, NY 10017.

British Library Cataloguing in Publication Data
Rayner, Claire
  Cottage Hospital. – New ed
  I. Title
  823.914 [F]

  ISBN 0-7278-4501-2

Typeset by Hewer Text Composition Services, Edinburgh.
Printed and bound in Great Britain by
Redwood Books, Trowbridge, Wiltshire.

INTRODUCTION
By Claire Rayner

Twenty-five or more years ago, I was a young would-be writer, trying to learn how to make my way in the world of books. I was writing for magazines and newspapers and I'd produced a couple of non-fiction books, but story-telling . . . that was a mystery to me. I knew I liked stories, of course; I've been an avid reader since before I was four years old and to this day I'm a pushover for a well-told tale. But how to tell a tale – *that* was the mystery.

So much so that it simply did not occur to me that I might be able to write fiction. But I was persuaded to try my hand. And because I knew that it is a basic rule of the learner writer always to write what you know, I opted to write about hospital life. After twelve years of sweat, starch, tears and bedpans as a nurse and then a sister in a series of London hospitals, I had an intimate knowledge of how such establishments work. I also knew that a great many people love peering behind closed doors into worlds they don't usually get the chance to experience.

So, I had a go. I started to tell myself stories of hospital life – rather romantic, but none the worse for that – only instead of keeping them in my own head as I had when I'd been a day-dreaming youngster, I struggled to put them on paper. And to my surprise and delight I found that publishers were willing to have a go, and gamble on me. They put my words into books – and I was delighted.

But also a bit embarrassed. I know it isn't an attractive trait to admit to, but there it is – I was a bit of a snob in those days. Not a social snob, you understand, but an intellectual snob. I had the notion that stories like these were a bit 'ordinary', that what really mattered was Literature with a capital 'L' and I knew perfectly well I wasn't writing that! So instead of using my own name on my first published attempts at story-telling, I borrowed my sister's first name and a surname from elsewhere in my family. And Sheila Brandon was born.

Now I am no longer a literary snob. I know that any storytelling that gives pleasure and interest to readers is nothing to be ashamed of and has a right to exist. It may not be Literature, but then what is? Dickens was just a story-teller in his own time, the equivalent of the writers of 'Eastenders' and 'Coronation Street'. Today he is revered as a Classic. Well, these stories of mine are never going to be classics, but I don't think, now I re-read them, that I need blush too much for them. So, here they are, the first efforts of my young writing years, under my own name at last. I hope you enjoy them. Let me know, either way!

Chapter One

The operating theatre was quiet, the big shadowless light above the table throwing a pool of clear radiance over the humped figure of the patient on the table and the bent heads of the two surgeons. In the shadows beyond the central pool of light, the little junior nurse padded softly from swab rack to trolley, from anaesthetic machine to sterilising room, her brown eyes absorbed in the task of the moment, her smooth young forehead creased a little as she concentrated.

Barbara, standing quietly at Daniel's side, putting instruments into his hand with automatic precision, felt happy. It was the sort of case she loved, she thought contentedly. An extra appendix put on at the end of the list, uncomplicated, and nothing but tidying up and off duty to come. And it was always nice to take Daniel's cases. She looked at the back of his head, at the line of dark red hair just showing beneath the green theatre cap, at the broad square shoulders, and smiled a little, under her mask. Quiet easy going Daniel, who never shouted at the nurse who scrubbed for him, who knew what he wanted to do and how to do it – he was comfortable to be with. And for Barbara that was one of the nicest things about him.

"Ten years," she thought, as she turned to her trolley

1

and started to thread the skin needles with nylon sutures. "Ten years I've known him – it's ridiculous – it can't be ten years since I came here – "

But it was. Ten years since she had first come to the Royal, a gawky nineteen year old, all legs and eyes, as Daniel had said the first time they had met.

Barbara slid into memory. She had been rushing across the courtyard from the Nurses' Home, her cape held round her with one hand, the other clutching desperately at the cap that refused to stay put on her silky black hair. She had careered head first into the big red-headed young man, the short white coat of the senior medical student straining across his wide shoulders.

"Here, hold on!" he'd cried in mock indignation. "You can't go around bashing medical students like that – we haven't enough to spare for that – " and he'd taken her cap from her, and pinned it securely on her head while she stood scarlet with mortification wishing the ground would open and swallow her up.

"There!" he'd said finally, standing back to admire the effect. "*That's* the way to wear those silly scraps of starch – it won't come off now – " He'd grinned at her red face then, and said with a voice bubbling with laughter, "We must be short of nurses at the Royal these days, if they're cradle-snatching babies like you to fill the school. You look like a young colt – all legs and eyes. How old are you?"

"Nineteen," Barbara had said defensively, trying to look it.

"I don't believe it," he'd said, his eyes glinting with amusement. "Not a day over sixteen – "

And they had both laughed, and Barbara had gone

2

on her way on duty feeling suddenly much happier. It had been lonely, those first weeks at the Royal, she remembered, turning round to put a needle holder in Daniel's outstretched hand. Daniel's easy friendship had helped her a lot, and she had come to watch for his big figure moving with deceptive laziness around the hospital. They had drifted into a companionable relationship, sharing the occasional free tickets to the theatre that came from Matron's office, going out together to celebrate on the day Daniel qualified, playing casual tennis with the rest of their small set of friends, thrilled for each other when one of them passed an exam, commiserating over the occasional setbacks. And if there had been a time, one hot long summer, when Barbara had found herself thinking of him as more than just a friend, she had learned to push those thoughts firmly away. He *was* a good friend – and that was all, she had told herself, when the mere sight of him had been enough to send her heart racing madly, enough to make her knees tremble with pleasurable fear. And he had never noticed, she thought gratefully, never seen the way I nearly made a fool of myself.

And now Barbara was the theatre Sister, no longer a leggy colt, but a tall and quiet woman with an air of serenity about her, wearing her smooth black hair in a neat chignon on which her snowy cap sat with authority. Daniel was the senior surgical Registrar, his Fellowship safely passed, and a brilliant future confidently prophesied for him by the consultant surgeons he worked for. There was some glinting white hair among the dark red at his temples now, and his face had settled into a craggy firmness that matched his powerful body.

"He must be – thirty-four now," Barbara thought, a little amused. "We're getting old – positively antique – "

Daniel started to put in the last of the skin sutures, as the anaesthetist at the head of the table turned off his machine. Another few minutes, and the patient would be on his way back to the ward, leaving Barbara and her junior free to tidy up and go off duty, and Daniel to his last ward round of the day.

As she started to prepare the skin dressing, Barbara grimaced a little. The gnawing pain that had been bothering her so slightly all afternoon was getting worse again – she'd better send the junior to find some milk as soon as they'd finished, she thought irritably. Damned pain – and she pushed the implications of the pain into the back of her mind, refusing to think about it.

"All done and dusted!" Daniel straightened his back, and looked across the table at his assistant. "Thanks, Jeff. Nice little job, wasn't it? Got it just in time – I thought it was just on a rupture – " and he nodded with obvious pleasure in the clinical judgement that had led him to time this operation so neatly.

"Very pretty, Dan. You fished it out a treat. I'd hate to have to play with a retro-caecal as inflamed as that little beauty." Jeff Peters pulled off his gloves, and stood back to let the porter lift the unconscious patient on to the trolley, watching them on their way out of the theatre, back to the ward. "Me for a quiet beer – it's been a long day. Join me?"

Daniel shook his head. "I'm on call, laddy. You'll have to swill on your own. Sister – " he turned to Barbara, " – about that gastrectomy tomorrow – "

He broke off sharply, and then leaned over to peer at Barbara more closely. She was standing beside her

4

trolley, grasping the edges with her gloved hands, her head bent.

"Barbara! What's the matter?" His voice was sharp with anxiety suddenly. "Are you ill again?"

Barbara hardly heard him. The pain under her ribs had suddenly flared, and the green tiled walls of the theatre had started to move, rotating and seeming to merge into shimmering gleams of light. Daniel's voice seemed to come muffled, from miles away, and she concentrated with every fibre of her being on standing still. "I won't faint," she told herself grimly, staring at a pair of forceps on the trolley beneath her hands in an effort to make the room stop moving. "I won't – "

Daniel's hard hands grasped her shoulders, and for a second, the walls steadied, and the blackness hovering at the edge of her vision receded. But then, as he gently pulled her back to lean against him, her willpower slid away from her, and she slipped into the blessed peace of oblivion.

When she opened her eyes again, she was lying in the big armchair in the surgeon's room, her mask pulled away from her face, her gloves and gown lying in a crumpled heap on the floor. Daniel was standing looming above her, holding a glass of warm milk, his face grim.

"Here you are." His voice was curt as he held out the glass to her. She tried to speak, but he glowered at her, and thrust the glass into her hand. Obediently, she took it, and began to sip.

Daniel stood at the window, his back to her, staring out at the light of the main ward block across the twilit courtyard. Barbara sat quietly after she had drunk the milk, the glass on her lap, waiting for the pain to recede,

5

too tired to attempt to speak. Outside she could hear the clatter of bowls and instruments and thought confusedly that she ought to go and help the junior clear up –

Ten minutes slid quietly by, and then she stirred experimentally and sat up, her hand automatically smoothing her hair.

"I'm sorry, Daniel," she said, her voice a little husky. "Stupid of me – "

"Bloody stupid!" His face blazed with anger as he whirled from the window and came to stand towering above her. "Has the pain gone now?"

She nodded, her head bent, unwilling to meet his eyes.

"You are without doubt the stupidest woman I know." His voice was still angry, but there was a hint of softening in it. "Are you trying to perforate that damn' ulcer of yours? Are you completely devoid of any common sense?"

Barbara pulled herself to her feet. "Look, I said I'm sorry," she said wearily. "I finished the case, didn't I? It isn't as though I flaked out in the middle – "

"That's got nothing to do with it," he said brusquely. "I told you three months ago when you first started to get symptoms of a peptic ulcer that theatre was too much for you – "

She stood very straight, and looked at him levelly. "See here, Daniel. I know you mean well. But I am *not* leaving the theatre, and that's that. This is my job, and I like it. If I've got an ulcer it's just one of those things. I was stupid today and I admit it – I hadn't time to go to lunch and that's why this happened. But it's the first sign of trouble I've had for weeks, and I'll make sure it doesn't happen again. But I told you

6

before and I'm telling you again. I'm not giving up my job – "

"For God's sake, Bar!" he ran his hands wearily across his face. "You know as well as I do that you ought to be working in a more peaceful atmosphere! The stress of theatre work is colossal, and you can't expect to do it well unless you are really fit. You got an ulcer because you work here, and if you go on in theatre with all the flap and bustle and the irregular meals, and all the rest of it, you might perforate and haemorrhage, and make a downright mess of yourself! It just isn't worth it." He came and stood beside her, taking her white face between his big hands.

"My dear, I know what it is to do the work you love. I'd be as miserable as hell if I had to give up surgery – but damn it all, your health's more important! Do something lighter for a year or so, and then you'll be fit enough to come back – "

Barbara set her mouth stubbornly. "No, Daniel! You're sweet to be so concerned, and I appreciate it. But this is my – my *life* and I'd be more than miserable if I had to give it up. So please, forget what happened this evening. I'll make sure I get my food regularly, and I'll take my pills and I'll be fine – "

He dropped his hands to his sides, and stood defeatedly staring at her. Then, he shrugged and turned and went, the door slamming behind him.

Barbara finished the evening's work with a sense of relief. She knew Daniel was right, but she felt she had convinced him with her refusal to listen to him. As she scrubbed instruments, and prepared for the next morning's lists, she remembered, unwillingly, what Sir

Peter Field had said when she had been sent to see him three months before.

"Duodenal ulcer, Sister – not good. You ought to leave that madhouse of a butcher-shop before you make an invalid of yourself. Come to one of the country branches, hmm?" But she had shaken her head, a little amused by his physician's prejudice against surgeons and operating theatres.

"I shall be all right, Sir," she had said quietly. "Diet and rest when I can. I'd be extremely unhappy to give up my post. It means a lot to me – "

Old Sir Peter had peered at her under his bushy brows and sighed gustily.

"Stubborn woman! All right then. But one more go like this last one and I'll see to it that Matron *makes* you take life easy. I'll put you on Probanthine now, anyway, and see you get the right food – but remember – I'm warning you – "

Well, she had had another go like the first one, this evening. Barbara scrubbed industriously at a pair of artery forceps and grimaced a little. There was no need for Sir Peter to know, she thought. I was silly today, but I won't let it happen again, so there's no need to report sick. No one need know.

But when she came on duty the next morning to find the second sister from the private theatres in her office, and a note asking her to report to Matron's office, her heart sank.

"Hi, Hughes," Dorothy Barker was pushing her thick fair hair under a tight green theatre cap. "What gives? Why the panic? Home Sister comes bustling over to me at the crack of dawn to say I'm to come here, and now this – " she gestured with her head at the note on

8

the green paper that Matron always used. "What's the matter?"

Barbara managed a smile. "Oh, I don't know," she said easily. "Probably there's a big job out at one of the country branches. I've had to do that before, if there isn't anyone there who can cope – "

Dorothy peered at herself abstractedly, her pug nose close to the little mirror. "Cripes, these bloody pimples! Theatre'll make a hag of me before I'm thirty – I daresay you're right. What have we got here?"

"Gastrectomy, exploration of abdominal mass – " They slid into rapid discussion of the morning's work, while Barbara ran through the details of the morning's lists, and re-arranged the staff off-duty so that Dorothy would have enough senior nurses to cover her. Then she smoothed her apron and powdered her nose, ready to go across to Matron's office.

As she combed her already immaculate hair, she stared at her reflection in the mirror. Dark brown eyes, set deep under straight brows, a high forehead, and cheeks shadowed under the high bones. "I look lousy," she admitted to herself miserably; "Lousy," and her eyes looked unhappily back at her, the skin under them smudged with violet shadows, the white skin taut over her temples.

Then she straightened her shoulders, pulled her black belt snugly around her waist, and smoothed her uniform over her slight hips. She was tall, and her slenderness enhanced her height, giving her an air of remote fragility that was very attractive. But it was true that now she did not look well – her face had that slightly muddy look that comes with too much work, and not enough time to relax before more work piles up.

Matron's office seemed ominously quiet to Barbara when she answered the cool "Come in!" and walked sedately across to the big desk.

Matron looked up at her, her usually stern face relaxing with pleasure.

"Nice to see you, Sister," she said cordially. "You've been so busy in the theatres lately, I seem to have missed you on my rounds. You're always scrubbed up when I put my head round the door. Sit down, my dear. You look tired," and she looked shrewdly at Barbara's face, clearly defined in the early morning light from the big window.

"Thank you, Matron," Barbara sat mechanically, her mind racing. Obviously, not a case at a country branch, or Matron would have said something immediately. What then?

Matron was leaning back in her chair, smiling at her. "Barbara Hughes," she said reminiscently. "I remember your first day here, my dear. So intense – so very shy – " She laughed. "You've grown up a lot since then, haven't you?"

Barbara was guarded. What was Matron getting at? "I'm nearly thirty, Matron," she said. "Time I grew up, I suppose."

"You have been happy at the Royal all these years?" The question came crisply.

Barbara raised an eyebrow, looking across at the older woman with directness.

"Why the past tense?"

Matron stood up, and came round to Barbara's side

of the desk and leaned against it as she rubbed her chin thoughtfully.

"Hmm. Straight question. All right – straight answer. You aren't well, are you?"

"I'm fine! Whatever made you think – ?" Barbara's voice was shrill with sudden anxiety.

"Oh don't try any fiddle-faddle with me, my girl." Matron was suddenly brisk. "You've got an ulcer, haven't you? And it's bothering you at the moment, isn't it? So I think the time has come for you to leave the theatres for a while – and, perhaps to leave the Royal – "

"Oh no!" Barbara's dismay was almost ludicrous in its intensity. "You aren't going to sack me, surely?"

Matron shook her head. "I couldn't possibly, my dear. You're much too good a Sister for that. But I hope to persuade you to see that you ought to go – for your own sake – just for a while."

"Oh, Matron!" Barbara slumped in her chair a little. "I've already been through all this with Daniel – Doctor Marston – I *like* theatre. I'm happy there. And as for leaving the Royal – I *couldn't*. It's my home – I've been here ten years!"

"I know, my dear. But all the same, it's time for you to make a change. You're too – insulated here. It isn't good for anyone to spend so long in one place, believe me – not at your age. And now you aren't really fit, the move becomes more than advisable. It's imperative. I'd be a pretty poor Matron if I let you make yourself really ill by keeping you on theatre. And that's what would happen."

Barbara bit her lip, angrily. "I suppose this is Daniel's doing," she said bitterly. "Interfering – "

11

"I wouldn't call a friend's concern for my well-being interfering," Matron said, her eyes crinkling a little. "He came to me because, I gather, you wouldn't listen to him. And he's been more than fair. He could have gone to Sir Peter, you know, and he's one of the old school. He'd have recommended that you be taken away from theatre, and I'd have been forced to do just that. This way, at least you have a chance to decide for yourself."

Barbara looked up, one eyebrow slightly raised: "Have I? Really?"

Matron laughed, gently. "I suppose not. But at least you can *pretend* this was your own idea. There won't be any record of the decision being forced on you."

"All right then," Barbara said unwillingly. "I know when I'm beaten. I suppose I'll have to ask for a transfer to another department – "

"No hope," Matron went back to her chair, and folded her hands crisply. "I told you, my dear – you need a complete change. There isn't a department in the Royal I'd send you to, in your state of health. What you need is a really quiet job – in a cottage hospital, perhaps – "

Barbara grimaced. "A cottage hospital! Have a heart, Matron! From the Royal to a cottage hospital? I'd die of boredom!"

"You wouldn't, you know," Matron sounded nostalgic, suddenly. "I started nursing in a cottage hospital, when I was seventeen – longer ago than I care to remember. It was delightful, that year I spent there. I think I learnt more about people and real nursing then than I learned in all the years of my training. It's quieter than a big teaching hospital like this, I grant you – and

12

from your point of view that's what matters – but it's far from boring."

Barbara stirred impatiently in her chair. "I'm sure you're right, Matron," she said with perfunctory courtesy, "but I just don't see myself working in a cottage hospital, somehow. I've lived in London for ten years now – all my friends are here – "

"You won't lose the real ones just because you leave London for a while. And you'll make some new ones. Now, look, my dear. You said a moment ago that you'd grown up – and it would be positively infantile to refuse to face the facts now. You aren't well, and a year at a quieter job now could save you months of real illness later, which would prevent you from working at all. Be your age, girl! See sense."

Barbara stood up, lifting her dark head to stare out of the big window across the busy traffic-roaring road. Then she sighed, sharply, and looked at Matron with a rueful smile on her delicate face.

"Put like that, what can I do? I'll have to give in gracefully, I suppose. I daresay I could get a job at Sandleas Cottage Hospital."

"Sandleas?"

"My sister lives there. Little place on the Kent coast, near Sandwich. One of those towns where everyone knows everybody else's business, and the hospital has all of thirty beds. You know?"

Matron nodded briskly. "What could be better? Sea air, someone to look after you, and a nice quiet place to work. And after a year or so, when you're quite fit again, we'll see about your coming back to the Royal. Let me know when you have everything settled, and in the meantime, I'll send another staff nurse to theatre

13

to take some of the load from you. Now, take the rest of the morning off duty to get this move organised – Sister Barker can carry on for a while." Barbara had nearly reached the door when Matron's voice called her back.

"And Sister – " Matron's eyes were quizzical, "Don't be too angry with Doctor Marston over this. I'd have found out sooner or later, you know, and the result would have been exactly the same. Better sooner than later, as it happens."

Barbara smiled at her, a wintry little smile, and then closed the door softly behind her to stand, for a moment, in the wide quiet corridor outside.

Behind her still face, she was seething with impotent rage. She had known Matron far too long and too well to argue with her when her mind was obviously made up, as it was over this business, but however calm and sensible Barbara may have seemed in the office, now she was furious. How dare Daniel run to Matron, telling tales like a silly schoolboy? Who did he think he was to interfere in her life in this high-handed fashion?

She pulled her cape round her shoulders more firmly, and with her head high, started down the corridor towards the doctors' common room. She picked her way over the buckets and mops that littered the corridor, past the little broom cupboard where a couple of maids were gossiping over an illicit cigarette, and put her head round the big door of the main sitting room.

Only Jeff, the House-Surgeon on Daniel's team, was there, sprawled in a big armchair behind a newspaper, his head wreathed in smoke from his smelly old pipe. He looked surprised when Barbara greeted him.

"Hello, Sister! You O.K. now? Gave me a proper

14

turn you did, passing out all funny like!" His mock cockney concern hid a real interest. "Mustn't do things like that, you know. Proper upsetting it was!"

"I'm fine, thanks, Jeff. Just hunger, that's all it was. Is Daniel around, do you know? I want a word with him."

Jeff lounged to his feet. "You're welcome to him this morning," he said, grimacing slightly. "He's in a foul temper. Marched off to the pool for a swim and told me I'd just bloody well have to cope on my own till lunchtime. Which is why I'm skulking here. If I go round the wards, everyone'll be asking questions only he can answer. I'm staying out of the way."

Barbara laughed a little grimly. "That's just fine. I'm in a temper too, so we should have an interesting discussion. Thanks, Jeff. I'll be seeing you."

She hurried over to her room, her head high. If Daniel thought he'd be able to avoid her by taking the morning off, he had another think coming, she told herself angrily, as she grabbed her swim suit and towel. He wasn't the only one who could find time for a swim this morning.

The little indoor pool a grateful ex-patient had presented to the staff of the hospital was quiet when she got there. She couldn't see Daniel at all, and the three medical students who were splashing around in the shallow end climbed out and made for the showers as she slipped into a cubicle and started to change.

When she came out, her tall body neatly encased in its sleek black suit, her hair tucked under a tight cap, there was no one at all in the water. The green tiles gleamed and shimmered, reflecting the slowly moving water in flashes of cool light. As she stood for a moment, poised

15

on the edge, Daniel suddenly appeared at the deep end, to stand staring down into the green depths, his face closed and grim. He hadn't seen her, and for a second she looked at him, at his muscular square body and flat abdomen, and in spite of herself and her anger, she thought, "He improves with his age – a handsome man – "

And then he lifted on his toes for a second, and went in, cleaving the water in a perfect dive. Immediately, Barbara followed suit, to come up a few feet from where Daniel was swimming strongly towards the far end of the bath.

"Good morning, Doctor Marston," Barbara's voice echoed loudly through the pool. "How *nice* to see you!"

He turned on his back and started to tread water.

"Barbara!" His surprise made him look ludicrous. "What are you doing here? Why aren't you on duty?"

She started to swim lazily towards the side, looking back at him over her shoulder. "Oh, I've all the time in the world," she said, her voice smooth, "I've been given the boot, you know, so what does an extra morning off matter?"

He frowned sharply, and followed her until they both reached the rail, to hold on to it, staring angrily at each other across the few feet of green water between them.

"The sack? I don't believe it," he said flatly.

"I didn't say the sack, did I? But I've got my marching orders all the same," Barbara said. "Matron thinks I should spend a year in a cottage hospital – to get my health right, I gather. And I also gather that I have *you* to thank for her solicitude."

He heaved himself out of the water to sit on the edge of the pool, staring down at her.

"You wouldn't listen to me," he said, his voice expressionless. "So I thought you'd listen to Matron. If you haven't the sense to see for yourself what you should do, then obviously someone else must *make* you do the right thing."

Barbara too pulled herself out of the pool to stand dripping beside him, her face grim as she looked down at him.

"And who do you think *you* are to decide what is the right thing for me? How dare you interfere in my affairs in this high-handed fashion?" Her voice was scathing. "You may have the power of life or death over your patients, Doctor Marston, but you certainly have no call to try to extend that power to me, I assure you. I am perfectly capable of making my own decisions."

"I am sure you are – except in this case it seemed to me that you were in considerable need of guidance."

"Did it indeed? Marston the omnipotent! You thought I needed guidance, and when I refused it, you made sure that your advice was forced upon me! Remarkable piece of medical practice!"

"I acted as a friend, not a doctor." His voice was low.

"I cannot see that you did anything of the sort," Barbara said icily. "Had you been the friend you profess to be, you would have known how much I wanted to stay in the theatres, and how much I would hate the idea of working anywhere but the Royal. There's one comfort in it all, I suppose – I won't have to see *you* again!" The cold dislike in her voice made him flinch for a moment, and then his face settled into its firm craggy lines again.

17

He stood up, and reached for his towel from the bench beside him.

"You are obviously much too emotionally disturbed over this to listen to reason," he said coldly. "So I won't attempt to offer any. I have no doubt that you will come to agree with me, when you've had time to simmer down a little."

"And I have no doubt that I will do nothing of the sort," Barbara flared, her face flushed with anger. "You are absolutely the most arrogant, unpleasant man I have ever met!"

"You haven't met enough men, then," he said, with a glint of humour. "Look, Barbara – I'm sorry you're so angry about this, but believe me, I acted for the best – and you *will* come to see that, really you will. In the meantime – where will you be going? I'd like to know – "

"And I'd rather you didn't! I don't want to see you again, Doctor Marston. You've done quite enough damage already, thank you. In future, I'll have the sense to keep well out of your way!"

And with a last angry stare at his face, she turned and ran to her cubicle. As she closed the door, she had a glimpse of him standing very still and straight at the edge of the pool, his towel held in one hand, his face stern and closed. When she came out again, her wet swim suit in her hand, he was gone. The pool was quiet and empty again, and as she stared across it she thought miserably, "I'll never swim here again, I suppose. And I won't see him again, either." And she wasn't sure whether the sense of desolation she felt was because of the loss of the Royal, or the loss of an old friendship.

Chapter Two

She stared out of the train window at the telegraph poles swooping past, at the green hedges blurred with speed, and let her magazine fall into her lap. Across the carriage, a woman with a fretful child crooned indistinctly in an effort to make the whining infant settle to sleep, and a man in the opposite corner rattled his newspaper irritably at the sound.

Barbara smiled a little, momentarily diverted, and then she turned back to the window and her thoughts. She felt curiously empty. It had taken all her willpower not to weep, the day before, when her nurses had shyly presented her with their leaving gift – a neat travelling clock. She had been swallowing her tears for four weeks, ever since she had made the final arrangements to leave the Royal, to go to Sandleas Cottage Hospital as a "Second Sister". But now she felt quite calm.

The letter from the Matron of the Cottage Hospital was in her bag, and she took it out to re-read it.

"I do hope you'll be happy here. I can't tell you how thrilled I am that you're coming to me. To have a Royal trained nurse is quite a feather in our caps anyway – there aren't many of you London girls who want to come to a quiet place like this – but to have Mrs.

Geoffrey Martin's sister on the staff is even more of an honour. I'm sure I'd like to offer you a room in our little Nurses' Home, but I realise, of course, that you'd much rather stay with your sister."

A most un-matronly letter, thought Barbara, as she slipped it back into its envelope. And she felt a little worried by the starry-eyed way the Matron wrote about "Mrs. Geoffrey Martin's sister". Barbara knew that Geoffrey was a fairly large frog in his little pond – but she hadn't realised how much Mary reflected his glory.

She started to think about Mary. She had been fourteen when Barbara had been born, and to the young Mary, her mother had been outrageous to present her with an infant sister after so many years of being an only child.

She had paid little attention to Barbara while she was growing up, and when Mary had married a young solicitor from Sandleas, the two had seen even less of each other, even after their parents had died, just after Barbara started training at the Royal.

Now, Mary was forty-three, and Geoffrey was forty-five, and their two children were growing up fast. "Jamie must be – sixteen now," thought Barbara, a little surprised. "Time goes so fast, and I haven't seen them for nearly two years now. Italy last holidays, and then they went to Spain the year before – " She slid deeper into reverie. "And Josie – she must be twelve – I wonder if Geoffrey's still the same – "

The train rattled over the points, and Barbara roused herself to grope on the rack for her two cases, to powder her nose and straighten her crumpled suit. Canterbury in five minutes. Geoffrey had promised to meet her

20

there with the car " – because the branch line is so tedious," Mary had written. "I'll see he meets your train, my dear. We're looking forward to seeing you, especially the children. And for heaven's sake, do stop all this nonsense about living at the hospital. I couldn't possibly permit it. I'd never be able to face people if my own sister was working in the town, and didn't live with me."

"Never mind what I'd like to do," thought Barbara a little wryly, as she peered out of the slowing train, trying to see Geoffrey's spare figure on the platform. "But I daresay it will be all right. And it's a very comfortable house."

The train ground agonisingly to a stop, and Barbara swung down on to the platform, stretching her cramped back a little as she looked around the bustling noisy station.

"Barbara!" There was real pleasure in the quiet voice behind her, and Barbara swung round to see Geoffrey smiling gently at her. His face was more heavily lined than it had been the last time she had seen him, she thought, but his crisp fair hair showed no trace of white. It still looked as though it had been crimped, so neat were the even waves that ran across his head. All his life his tightly curling hair had been an embarrassment to him, and especially after he qualified. As a solicitor, carefully climbing the ladder of success, he had to look the part, so he kept his rebellious hair cut short and brutally brushed close to his head. His rather pale blue eyes, a little too large for his thin face, were tired too, Barbara thought, but he still held himself very erect, his neat black suit sitting prim and spotless across his narrow shoulders.

21

"Geoffrey!" she said, as he kissed her cheek with a polite brotherly peck. "How kind of you to meet me here. I could have taken the branch line quite easily – "

He picked up her bags and started urging her gently towards the barrier, part of his attention on her, part of it concentrating on finding a porter.

"Not at all, my dear," he said. "Mary would have been most upset to think of you putting up with that dreadful train – and so would I. It's a bare half-hour's drive, you know, and nearly three times that by rail – ah, porter!"

They found Geoffrey's car across the big station yard, and Barbara settled herself gratefully into its luxurious comfort.

"How long have you been running a Jaguar?" she asked, as Geoffrey slammed the door on his side and fiddled with the ignition key. "Did you get tired of the Rover?"

"No – I was quite fond of the old Rover, really." He sounded a little regretful. "But people seem to expect me to run a fancy job like this, so Mary settled on a Jag. But it's very comfortable, I must say."

As the big car ate the miles, they talked desultorily of London theatres, of Jamie's progress at school, of Josie and her dancing and riding classes, and gradually Barbara relaxed. This was a life she knew so little about, she thought. In all the years at the Royal, she had lost touch with the comfortable affluent existence her sister enjoyed. Once, she would have been impatient of it, but now, feeling not quite as well as she might, there was a powerful pull in the thought of real comfort, of a warm well run house, of all the extra things that money could provide. Barbara had never really cared much for possessions, but somehow, riding in this silent, richly comfortable car, she felt the insidious attractions of owning such pleasant objects.

"You've changed." Geoffrey's voice cut across her musing. "Two years isn't all that long, really, but you're different, somehow – "

Barbara smiled. "I can't think why," she said lightly. "I've been living the same sort of life for the past two years as I did before. Nothing's happened to me to make me any different. Just older."

He smiled crookedly at her, taking his attention momentarily from the road. "It suits you – the change, I mean. You're more – serene than I remembered."

"My dear Geoffrey! You hardly ever had time to notice me at all!" Barbara said. "Whenever I've visited Sandleas you've been too busy at the office to see much of me!"

He laughed shortly, "I don't spend much time in living, do I? Always work. I feel a bit like Alice sometimes – you know, running like hell to keep in the same place – "

Barbara looked at him in some surprise. This was a new Geoffrey. "I thought you liked work?"

"Oh, I do! It's just that sometimes – oh, well," he grinned a little crookedly again, and lapsed into silence.

The car purred on, and Barbara sat wondering a little about the man beside her. She had never paid much attention to him. He was Mary's husband, and Jamie's and Josie's father, and beyond that, seemed to have little personality of his own. Perhaps, she thought, I've been unfair to him. I've never thought much about him

23

at all, as a person. Or about him as Mary's husband, if it comes to that. Is theirs a happy marriage? The thought slid into her mind, and she pushed it away. Whether they were happy or not, it was no business of hers. She and her sister, and her sister's family, had lived at arm's length from each other for the whole of their lives. This was no time to start getting involved with them on an emotional level, now she was to live with them.

"It'll be odd, living in an ordinary household after all those years in a Nurses' Home," she said suddenly.

"I hope you'll like it," Geoffrey said. "The children are delighted, you know. They're awfully proud of you."

"Proud of me?" Barbara said wonderingly. "Why on earth – ?"

"Oh, they're rabid hospital fans. Josie especially. She never misses a hospital programme on TV, and she reads hospital novels till they come out of her ears. She thinks it's marvellous to have an aunt who's a trained nurse, and a theatre sister at that."

Barbara made a little face. "She'll be a bit disappointed with my new job, then. As far as I can tell, I'm to be a general dog's-body."

"How do you mean?"

"Well, the hospital has thirty beds – you know, probably?"

He shook his head. "Mary knows more about it than I do. She's on the management committee."

"So *that's* why Matron was so pleased about having Mrs. Geoffrey Martin's sister on the staff!"

"I daresay she is. Mary's quite a VIP in Sandleas nowadays – she feels it's good for my practice if she's on all the local committees and what-have-you.

But what about the job? Why are you so dreary about it?"

"I don't mean to sound dreary," Barbara said hastily. "It's just so different from anything I'm used to. Apparently there's Matron, and a second Sister – that's me – who does everything from running the wards to ordering the stores and coping with the whole hospital when Matron's off duty, a couple of staff nurses, and a collection of very young pre-training cadets and part-time assistant nurses. So it isn't very glamorous, I'm afraid, even from Josie's point of view."

"She'll find it glamorous enough, don't worry. Jamie too. He's decided to do medicine, by the way. Did you know?"

"Really? I supposed I'd assumed he'd follow you."

"Mary would have liked him to, I think – actually, she wanted him to read for the Bar. But he's a determined boy, in some ways. He'll do what he wants to do, not what other people think he should. More like Mary than me."

"I wonder why he chose medicine?"

Geoffrey chuckled a little wickedly. "Because his mother fancied law, I suspect." He turned the car into the wide gates that fronted the house. "Here we are. I'll dump your bags for you, but forgive me if I don't come in with you, Barbara. I've got a client coming to see me at the office in ten minutes. I'll see you again at dinner – and I shall look forward to that. It's good to have you with us."

"Thank you, Geoffrey," Barbara said warmly. "It's sweet of you to make me feel so welcome."

"I mean every word of it." He looked at her for a

25

moment, his tired face lightening with a smile. "Every word of it."

He put her cases down on the polished red tiles of the broad doorstep, and with a brief wave he was gone, the big car turning smoothly on the gravel drive.

Barbara smiled at the woman in the print overall who was waiting by the door she had opened in response to the sound of the car. "Hello, Mrs. Lester," she said. "Remember me? I saw you last time I was here."

"Indeed I do, Miss." The woman picked up the cases. "Nice to see you again. Mrs. Martin's upstairs. I'll tell her you're here."

Barbara stood in the wide hallway, slowly pulling off her gloves, and looked around her. The white paintwork gleamed in the morning sunlight, and the red carpet was thick under her feet. There was a huge bowl of beautifully arranged daffodils and hyacinths on the low table in the centre, and the flowers were reflected in the high polish of the surface. She could smell coffee, and the faint redolence of polish, and a hint of the sea that was so near. The house felt warm, and rich, and comfortable, and Barbara sighed with real pleasure.

"Barbara!" Mary's voice floated down the wide stairs. "I'm up here, my dear. Come up!"

"Coming!" Barbara climbed the stairs, stopping for a moment at the window half-way up to bury her nose in another bowl of flowers. The door of Mary's room was half open, and Barbara went in, her feet sinking into the pale Indian carpet that covered the floor.

Mary was sitting at her dressing table, almost dressed, the jacket of her suit lying ready on the peach silk counterpane of her bed. She was carefully painting

26

her mouth as Barbara came in, and she smiled stiffly at Barbara through the mirror.

"Just let me finish this – " she spoke through stretched lips as she plied her lipstick. "Then let me look at you – "

Barbara sank into the armchair at the side of the dressing table and looked at her sister. She had the same thick dark hair that Barbara had, except that it was streaked, here and there, with white, and the same dark brown eyes. But where Barbara's face was clear cut, with the skin stretched tightly across the cheekbones, Mary's face was blurred a little with fat, the clean lines of her bones hidden with flesh. There were deep lines between her eyes, and each side of the nose and mouth, but her skin was good, showing clearly the expensive care that was lavished on it.

After a moment, she swung round in her chair and smiled at Barbara.

"Well, my dear! And how are you! Feeling better?"

Barbara stretched a little. "I'm not ill," she said defensively, feeling some of the old hostility rise, the hostility she always found Mary could make her feel. "Just in need of a change."

"I've known that for years," Mary said briskly. "But you wouldn't listen. But now you're here, we must see you get plenty of rest. I'm very pleased you're staying with us, Barbara."

"There's no need for me to impose on you, Mary," Barbara said. "I could easily live at the hospital – "

"My dear, do stop talking like that. I wouldn't dream of it. That poky little Nurses' Home! We have plenty of room here, and there's not the least need for you to live anywhere else. And it's no imposition, because we've plenty of help. Mrs. Lester comes every day, and I pay her quite enough for her to look after another person. So that's that." She stood up, and started to put her jacket on. "Look, my dear. I'm sorry to have to leave you alone on your first morning, but I have a wretched meeting to go to – The Pageant of the Women's Institute is next month, and if I don't chase them up, nothing gets done. I'll be back for lunch, so you unpack, and take things easy till then. The children are out, too, so you'll be left in peace." She kissed Barbara briefly, and made for the door.

"You have the same room as the last time you were here – and you can share the children's bathroom – do you mind?"

Barbara followed her out on to the wide upper landing.

"Not in the least. I'm used to sharing a bathroom with far more than two people, you know." She smiled. "And from what I remember of the children, they don't exactly haunt the bathroom!"

Mary frowned fleetingly. "Well, they aren't children any more, not in that sense," she said. "But even so, you should manage. Mrs. Lester!" She stood in the downstairs hall, pulling on her gloves. "Mrs. Lester – ah, there you are! Take Miss Hughes' bags up, will you, and make her some coffee? And don't forget – we need three loaves from the baker, and 'phone the butcher for me. All right, Barbara? See you at one." And she was gone. Barbara stood at the door for a moment, watching her sister drive her own small car out of the drive.

"She drives as she is," she thought, smiling a little to herself. "Efficient – quick – thorough," and then she turned to look at the hall again.

Mrs. Lester padded upstairs with her cases, and Barbara followed her, enjoying the sense of peace and comfort the house wrapped around her.

Her room was a big one. As Barbara looked round at it she said, "It looks different – "

Mrs. Lester nodded. "Mmm. Mrs. Martin, she had the decorators in, and one of those designer people from London. Turned everything upside down, she did. But it's very nice, I daresay."

It was. The room was in shades of blue, from the deep midnight of the carpet, through the lighter blue of the flowered curtains and counterpane, to the pale walls.

"Even the sheets and blankets is blue," said Mrs. Lester, following Barbara's gaze round the room. "Very modern and all that. Mind you, I couldn't fancy anything but white sheets myself. Seems unnatural to me, coloured sheets." She bustled about the room, opening drawers and wardrobe ready for Barbara to unpack. "But I daresay it's all what you're used to. Mrs. Martin – her sheets and blankets are peach, and Josie's – hers are a yellow, like primrose." She chuckled. "Jamie though – he had a right row about his. His mother fancied green for him, but he wasn't having any. He said if he couldn't have white, he'd have khaki, so that was that. He's a terror, that boy."

Barbara smiled a little uncomfortably. "Boys often are – " she said vaguely, opening the first of her cases. She didn't like the way Mrs. Lester lingered at the door, looking for a chance to gossip. "This won't take me long," she went on, trying to avoid seeming unfriendly. "I'll be down in a minute."

"All right, Miss." Mrs. Lester started to go. "I'd better get on, I daresay. There's a lot of people for tea this afternoon – to meet you – and I've got some baking to do. I'll have your coffee ready soon."

Barbara was aware of a faint sense of annoyance as she put her neatly folded clothes away in the prepared drawers. Mary might have asked her if she wanted a tea party, she thought crossly. How like her not to mention it.

Her unpacking took very little time, and she washed in the cool white bathroom between her own room and Josie's before going downstairs.

She could hear the radio in the kitchen, blaring away as Mrs. Lester hurried round her baking, so Barbara went into the big drawing-room that overlooked the wide garden at the back of the house. This room, too, showed the hand of "designer people from London". It was wide, and long, and the chintz and dark mahogany furniture Barbara remembered had given way to modern square couches and chairs, and bleached wood, with the same kind of one-colour scheme Barbara's bedroom had. She looked round at the purple carpet, the amethyst curtains, the deep lilac walls, the pale lavender cushions, and sighed a little. "It's like a furniture shop window," she thought with amusement. "Too perfect for words."

But the chairs were comfortable, and the room felt restful. On an impulse, she wandered across the hall to the dining-room, to see what the designers had done there. Here, there was red and mahogany, rich and warm, redolent of good food and wines. But, when Barbara put her head round the door of the little room overlooking the drive, which Mary called the library, she was even more amused. This was Geoffrey's special room, she knew, and here it seemed

Geoffrey had unexpectedly displayed some of his son's will. The room hadn't changed at all. There was still the big, rather battered desk, the brown carpet, the green upholstered chairs Barbara remembered from previous visits. A room with quiet character of its own – "Not in the least like a shop window," Barbara told herself, smiling a little.

It was the telephone on the desk that made her think, for a moment. Then she went across to it, and looked up the hospital 'phone number in the big directory.

She dialled the number with a quizzical expression on her smooth face. "As Mary hasn't told me about the tea party," she thought, a little wickedly, as she waited for the hospital to answer, "she can't expect me to be here – ". She heard an answering voice on the line. "May I speak to Matron, please? – Matron? Good morning. This is Barbara Hughes. I know I'm not starting duty till next Monday, but I thought perhaps I'd come and introduce myself in advance – This afternoon, perhaps? – fine. About three, then. Why, yes, thank you. I'd love to have tea – good-bye till then."

As she hung up, she felt a twinge of guilt. Mary, after all, meant well, she thought. Perhaps it was wrong of her to make an alternative arrangement. But then her face hardened. "Mary isn't going to run my life, even if I am living in her house," she told herself firmly. "And if I don't start on the right foot, I won't have a hope in hell."

Lunch was a fairly pleasant meal. The children came home from school for it, and greeted her joyously. Josie, in particular, hung on to her aunt's hand, looking up into Barbara's face adoringly, her pale blue eyes,

31

so like her father's, full of heroine-worship. Jamie had greeted her gruffly, but with real pleasure under his sixteen-year-old gaucheness. Mary was gracious and talked smoothly of her morning with the committee, of the pageant that was to come, of the stupidity of the various members of the committee, stopping occasionally to tell Josie to take her elbows from the table, or to tell Jamie to eat more slowly.

Jamie, after one of these remonstrances, winked briefly at his aunt, his brown eyes merry and glinting a little with wickedness. Mary affected not to notice this, or to notice the way he then ate with exaggerated slowness, even though it meant that he kept them all waiting for their pudding while he meticulously finished his cutlet.

Barbara found herself watching her niece and nephew as Mary's conversation ran smoothly on. Josie, her fair hair cut into a long swinging bob, was quiet, a little withdrawn, watching her mother's face anxiously after she had been told to take her elbows from the table. "Like me, a little," Barbara thought, warming to the frail little body. "Hates to be in any sort of trouble – I was like that." Jamie, on the other hand, for all his adolescent awkwardness, had an air of strength about him that Barbara hadn't noticed before when he was younger. His hands and wrists stuck bonily out of his sleeves, with a promise of power that would develop, in time. But it was his personality that was strongest of all. He said little, but when he looked at his mother at one point, after she had said something rather scathing about one of her fellow committee members, with something very like scorn in his deep-set eyes, Barbara shivered a little, involuntarily. "I'd hate to be in his bad

32

books," she thought, a little surprised at her reaction to him. "He could be a bad enemy."

When the children had gone back to school, and Mary and Barbara sat over their coffee, Mary said suddenly:

"Barbara – why aren't you married?"

Barbara stared at her, her eyebrows raised a little. "Why? Because I don't choose to be," she said as repressingly as she could. Mary ignored the hostility in her sister's voice.

"But you should be, you know. You must be – nearly thirty, now. Time you settled down."

Barbara lit a cigarette, trying to hide her annoyance.

"I can't think why you should imagine that marriage is the only way a woman can settle down," she said as lightly as she could. "I have a very absorbing career. I'm perfectly happy with it."

"Oh, a career." Mary dismissed it with a wave of her well-manicured hand. "That's all very well. But a woman needs more than that. A home and security – children. *That's* a real career."

"I can't say I fully agree with you." Barbara let her annoyance show.

"No, there's no need to get huffy, Barbara. It's just that I have your best interests at heart – and *I'm* sure you should marry. What about that man you used to mention last time you were here – Daniel something? What's his background?"

"I am not in the least interested in Daniel's background, and I am not in the least interested in marrying him, if that's what you're meaning. He is merely a friend," Barbara was icy.

"Friends are all very well, my dear. But a husband is

more to the point. Now, there are several men I know, all of whom are doing very well for themselves – "

Barbara stood up. "Look, Mary, let's understand each other. I am not in Sandleas to be toted around your marriage market. I am here to do a job of work, until I am ready to return to London and the Royal. So please, don't run away with the idea that you can do anything to alter that. You insist that I stay here – and I will. But on my terms." She looked at her sister firmly, her face flushed a little.

Mary looked back at her, the line between her eyes accentuated. "Must you be so – direct? I have no intention of toting you, as you put it. I merely wanted to help you – "

"You started by pretty direct yourself, didn't you?" Barbara said coldly. "And as for helping me – you must try to see I don't need any help – not of that sort, anyway. I just want to be left in peace, that's all."

Mary stood up too, and after a moment, said, "I'm sorry, my dear. I suppose I was a bit abrupt. I didn't mean to upset you – but I do so want to see you with the same comfort I have. You have to work so hard – "

Barbara softened, and put her hand impulsively on the older woman's arm.

"I'm sorry too, Mary. I shouldn't be so touchy. I do understand, I suppose – but I want you to understand me. And as for work – well, I'm used to it. And I like it."

"Don't you like comfort too?"

Barbara looked round the warm dining room. "I suppose I do," she said slowly. "But if it isn't for me, there it is. You can't just walk into it, can you?"

Mary smiled a little. "No – but you can walk in the

right direction. That was what I meant. Wouldn't you like – this?" The sweep of her arm included everything. The warm comfortable house, the security of her marriage, her two handsome children – even Mrs. Lester washing dishes in the sink.

Barbara bit her lip. "I would, I suppose," she said again unwillingly. "I daresay there *are* times I would happily change places with you – but if I can't, I can't. Look, Mary, let's not talk about this any more. I've had a long day, and I've got to go to the hospital now – "

"The hospital? But I have some people coming to tea, to meet you – " Mary sounded angry again.

"Oh, really?" Barbara's voice was smooth. "I wish you'd told me earlier. I've arranged to go to see Matron this afternoon. What a pity," and she avoided Mary's eye as the lie slipped out so easily.

"I'll ring Matron now and explain," Mary was making for the door. "She won't mind – "

"But I would, Mary." Barbara stood very still in the centre of the room. "I made an arrangement and I intend to keep to it. I'm sorry."

The sisters stared at each other for a second, then Mary smiled. "I see," she said softly. "I see. Well – could you try to be back before four, perhaps? I've invited these people specially – it will be rather embarrassing for me – and a little insulting to them, don't you think?"

Barbara bit her lip. Put like that, Mary had her pinned, like a moth. "All right," she said unwillingly. "I'll try. But another time, Mary, tell me your plans in advance, when they affect me, will you? I do have arrangements of my own, you know. I'm not one of the children."

Mary smiled again, triumphantly this time. "Of course I will, Barbara," she said silkily. "And again, please forgive me. I keep forgetting how adult you are. Fourteen years seniority sometimes blinds me to it."

Barbara escaped the house with a sense of real relief. She knew that Mary's and her own will clashed easily, but she hadn't realised quite how soon the clash would come.

"And I'm supposed to be here to rest," she told herself bitterly, as she turned out of the drive, towards the town centre. "This next year isn't going to be easy, something tells me – "

Chapter Three

By the time Monday arrived, bringing her first day on duty at the Cottage Hospital, Barbara felt like a violin string. Her nerves were stretched to breaking point, and keeping her temper had become the most difficult thing she had ever had to do.

It wasn't that she wasn't made comfortable in Mary's house – she was. Everything that could contribute to her comfort was provided, from early morning tea to fresh flowers in her room every day. The children were obviously delighted to have her there, and Josie, in particular, spent every moment she could with her aunt. She would sit curled up on Barbara's bed, watching her comb her long hair, saying nothing, her big eyes fixed unblinkingly on Barbara's face. And while Barbara sat sewing, or reading, or writing letters, Josie would sit beside her, content just to be in her company. Jamie too made her feel happy, treating his aunt to his rare smiles, and occasionally asking her for help with his school homework. Geoffrey she hardly saw, as he came in only for meals, and then incarcerated himself in his own shabby library to work long into the night. But when he did meet her around the house or at meals, his abstracted face would break into a warm smile, and he would murmur. "Everything all right? Feeling better? Good!" before sinking back into his private thoughts.

It was Mary who was the problem. Her personality was so much the strongest in the household that she made herself felt even when she was just sitting – a rare occurrence – and reading. The whole house seemed to relax and stretch itself with a sigh of relief when she went out to one of her many committee meetings, and Barbara felt guilty when she, too, was glad to see her sister's car turning out of the drive. Mary was charming and friendly, and said no more about her plans to introduce her sister to eligible men, but Barbara felt that this was the calm before the attack. She was constantly on the defensive, waiting for Mary to say or do something wrong, and the fact that she didn't only made the tension in Barbara greater. So much so, that Barbara found herself reacting to Mary's simplest remarks with cool caution rather than sisterly affection.

On the Sunday evening before she was to start work, Barbara spent an hour in her bedroom preparing her uniform for the next morning. Josie, as usual, sat with her, silent, watching Barbara's deft fingers make up a frilled cap and put the buttons into her uniform dress. Barbara watched the child covertly, and smiled a little at the concentration on the pale little face as Josie tried to follow each step in cap-making.

"I wish she were mine – " The thought slid into her mind unbidden and, almost with panic, Barbara tried to push it back. But she couldn't. She loved Josie, and Jamie, and she *did* wish they were her children. She wished she could be the person who could make Josie the happy chattering child she ought to be, instead of

38

the silent, nervous scrap she was. And she wished too, that the house, the comfortable warm house that was so attractive, was hers, also.

Her fingers stopped their work, and fell into her lap, and Barbara sat staring out of the window, her face abstracted.

"I suppose Mary's right, in a way. I do want all this – the security of marriage, the comfort of a husband and children – I suppose that's why I got so angry when she said so – it hurt – "

"What are you thinking about, Auntie Bar?"

Josie's voice shattered her thoughts. "Mmm?" Barbara bent her head to her cap again. "Thinking about? Oh, nothing very much. About – people I know."

"I wish I was you," Josie said suddenly, after a pause.

"Why, darling? It's much nicer to be twelve, really it is – all sorts of exciting things to come – "

Josie stretched her legs in front of her, and stared at her feet.

"Oh nothing exciting will happen to me. I'll just get married, I suppose – "

"Wouldn't that be exciting?"

"I don't think so – I'd much rather be a nurse, like you. I think being married must be awful. Having to tell people what to do all the time."

Barbara's face creased with pain, suddenly, as she stared at the solemn child on the bed. "I hate Mary," she thought viciously. "I hate her – to let a child think marriage is just that – "

But she smoothed her face, and tried to speak lightly. "Oh, darling, it isn't like that at all, really. Married people do have to tell people what to do sometimes, but not all the time – "

39

"Mummy does," Josie's voice brooked no argument. "Auntie Bar, do you like Mummy?"

Barbara felt sick for a moment. Had her hostility to her sister been so obvious? "Of course I do, sweetheart. Mummy is my sister. Of course I like her – "

"I don't think you do, really." Josie raised her head and looked at her. "Do you know what? I think you're like me. You wish Mummy would go away – Do you know what else? I wish Mummy would go away and *you* were here for always instead – "

"Josie! Stop it! You mustn't say things like that – it's – It's dreadful – "

"I don't care!" Josie's voice rose shrilly. "It's true. I *hate* Mummy – I love *you*. I wish you were my mother!"

Barbara took Josie's narrow shoulders and shook her gently, trying to damp down the hysteria rising in the child's voice.

"Josie, listen to me. You're – you mustn't say things like that. Mummy loves you a lot, and that's why she – she has to tell you what to do and what not to do. You don't bother to tell things like that to people you don't love. Girls of your age always get cross with their mothers – it's part of growing up. But if you say things like that, you'll feel dreadful afterwards, when you aren't angry with your mother any more. Don't you see?"

Josie's soft mouth trembled a little, and then settled stubbornly into a line. "No I don't," she said flatly. "I *do* wish you were here all the time instead of Mummy – "

Barbara's hands dropped, and she looked down at the bent fair head with a feeling of defeat.

40

"Why are you so angry with your mother, Josie?" she asked after a long moment.

Josie shrugged. "I'm not specially angry – " she muttered.

"Yes you are," Barbara said gently. "You must be, or you wouldn't have said that to me. Now, tell me what it is."

Josie raised her head, and looked at her aunt, her eyes stormy. Then her face crumpled, and she said, "I said I wanted to be a nurse, like you, and she said – she said – " Tears started to fall down her face.

"What did she say, love?" Barbara sat down beside her, and put an arm round her shoulders. "What happened?"

Josie leaned gratefully on her aunt, and gulped a little. "She said no daughter of hers was going to be a skivvy for anyone – she said – she said – she didn't want me turning into a – a dreary spinster like you –" The child's shoulders started to shake with huge sobs. "And you're not! You're not dreary – I love you, Auntie Bar, really I do – and I *hate* Mummy!" and she abandoned herself to uncontrolled weeping, throwing her thin arms across Barbara in an ecstasy of tears.

Barbara sat rigid, staring across the room above the child in her lap, and her anger rose in a sick cold wave inside her. She wanted to cry too, like Josie, but her rage was too deep for tears. While part of her mind repeated with heavy monotony. "How dare she? How dare she? – " another part argued. "But she's right, isn't she? You want to be married, like Mary, don't you? You want her life for yourself – her house – her marriage – her children – "

Later that evening, after she had settled Josie into

41

bed with a hot drink, Barbara stood in the darkened bedroom, looking down on the exhausted sleeping face on its primrose coloured pillow, and sighed. Josie felt better now, she knew, having poured out her anger and resentment against her mother.

"She'll forget it," she told herself optimistically. "It's just part of adolescence – " But she knew that whatever happened to Josie's feelings, her own were too deeply lacerated to recover very quickly. Josie had said what Barbara herself hadn't dared to put into words. To have been shown her own private and, to Barbara, wrong thoughts, by a child – that hurt desperately.

"One thing's certain," Barbara told herself as she quietly closed the door on the sleeping child in the pretty frilly yellow room. "I *must* make an effort to be more friendly to Mary. I can't let myself show my feelings before the children so clearly – "

She was glad that Mary and Geoffrey were out, glad that Jamie had gone to a school play. "If they had been in," she thought, "the whole thing would have boiled over into something quite dreadful. As it is, no one but Josie and I know about it – "

So, when Monday morning came, she was relieved. With work to occupy her mind, she wouldn't be able to brood so much on her feelings and problems with her relationship with Mary. Work was the best therapy she knew.

Much to her surprise, she fell in love with the hospital. It was a converted manor house, and there were still unexpected steps up and down, odd corners that clearly showed the origins of the house, and the place had an atmosphere that was comforting.

Matron showed her around properly on that first

42

morning on duty. She was a bustling, fat, happy woman, whose tongue was never still, who wore her uniform with an air of "Lawks-a-mussy-me-this-is-none-of-I."

To Barbara, used to the super-efficient Matron of the Royal, who looked as though she had been born in her uniform, this Matron came as a rather pleasant change. Matron Elliott was for all the world like an old-fashioned children's nanny, with her big soft bust, her billowing hips spreading widely under her tight black belt, her well-polished old black shoes pushed out of shape by bunions. Her hair was iron grey and curled in wild tendrils that she was forever pushing under the edge of the big old-fashioned white veil that she wore.

"What a pretty uniform that Royal one is, isn't it, Sister Hughes? I do like the wide skirts so much – and that pretty frilly cap – you'll be a real ornament about the old place, really you will. Now, here's our men's ward. Twelve beds, you see, and nearly always full, every one of them – it's a nice ward, isn't it? It was the library of the old house – that's why it's so cosy, I think – Mr. Hunniset, you know you shouldn't be out of bed at this time of the morning, now – what? Oh well, hurry along then, and no smoking in the lavatory, mind – Ah, Nurse Field! Here is Sister Hughes – if you need any help, just ask her, won't you – " Barbara nodded a little breathlessly at the young assistant nurse in her lilac dress and butterfly cap, before Matron swept her inexorably on her way. She barely had time to look at the bright little men's ward, with its panelled walls painted in cream, the red counterpanes on the dozen beds, the men who peered curiously at her over their morning newspapers.

43

"This is the women's ward, now. Twelve beds again, nearly all medical cases, though we do the odd bit of surgery – this was the drawing-room of the old house – that's why it has so many windows – do you like the curtains? They were a gift from your sister – very generous to us, is Mrs. Martin – Good morning Mrs. Innes! How's the chest this morning? Better? – good – ah, Nurse Morgan – here is Sister Hughes. You'll find her a great help if you need any – Nurse trained at the Royal Dover Hospital, Sister – a local girl – getting married soon, aren't you, Nurse? – "

Barbara smiled at the blushing blonde staff nurse, and the large, panting woman she was helping out of bed into a wheelchair, and then followed Matron on her way through to the end of the ward.

"Now!" Matron pushed open the door at the end, and stood back to smile at Barbara as she pushed her hair under her veil for the umpteenth time. "Here is our children's ward. Just the four cots, you see, and very nice, don't you think?"

It was delightful. A room with a glass wall all down one side, overlooking a lawn starred with daffodils and with a couple of venerable elm trees to give shade. The four cots were pushed against the walls, and in the centre of the room a big play pen held a couple of fat babies. In two of the cots another couple of toddlers sat pulling dolls to pieces, one of them with chocolate smeared happily over his face, the other wearing, very solemnly, a bandage over one ear.

A coal fire burned cheerfully behind a high Victorian fireguard, and a middle-aged woman in the uniform of an assistant nurse stood in one corner busily ironing babies' nightdresses. It was more like a private nursery than a hospital ward. Matron, with a flick of her skirts that displayed an expanse of black-stockinged leg surmounted by dark green bloomers, hopped over the edge of the playpen and squatted down beside the babies, hugging them to her ample bosom in an expansive loving gesture. They squealed with pleasure, and climbed all over her, while Barbara stood and laughed delightedly at the whole charming picture.

"I love these two," Matron said happily. "We've had 'em three months now – cousins they are, live in the same house. Their mothers are in the San – primary TB's. But the babies are very happy with us, aren't they, Nurse Baker? This is Sister Hughes – "

They continued their tour, covering the same parts of the hospital Barbara had seen on her first visit on the day she had arrived in Sandleas, but this time Matron told her all the duties she would have to do as they went along.

As Barbara had suspected, she was to be a sort of general factotum. She was to supervise the three little wards, and the two private rooms, take charge of the Casualty Department, and look after the minute operating theatre. "We don't get much here, I'm afraid. The odd appendix, occasional hernia – you know. Mind you, we've had our moments of excitement. We got a Polish sailor last year, with a cerebral abscess – took him off his boat at the Goodwins they did, and couldn't get him any further than here. So the neuro-surgeon came down from Canterbury, and very nice he was too. The man did very well, and the nurse on the male ward picked up quite a bit of Polish before he went back home – they flew him out, from Dover. And we sometimes get accident cases, of course, especially in the summer – all the holiday people, you know. Very careless they are, silly things."

They continued their tour in the hospital kitchens. These seemed hardly to have changed from the old manor house days. The range had been replaced with a modern electric cooker, and there was an incongruous huge white refrigerator, but the floor was still of the old stone flags, and the big centre table was scrubbed whitewood. Matron perched herself on a corner of it, and she and Barbara sipped the cups of coffee provided by the thin harassed-looking woman who was the only cook.

"You saw upstairs when you were here the other day, of course. It's a nice little Nurses' Home, isn't it? Mind you, nice rooms though they are, it's a bit of a nuisance living right *in* the hospital, as it were. Every time I drop something on the floor, I'm afraid of waking the babies underneath! But they seem to be used to it – they never wake up!" and she laughed comfortably and drank her coffee with slightly noisy enjoyment.

Barbara felt herself warming to this unorthodox hospital and its matron. The people who worked in it were obviously happy to be there. Matron herself, with her warm, overflowing personality, and real shrewdness under her apparent chattering inconsequence, was the sort of person who could become a good friend. Barbara felt her spirits lifting. Even if she was having trouble settling to the idea of living with Mary, work was going to be very pleasant. "And that's the important thing," Barbara told herself.

"I'm sure you're very lucky to be living in that lovely house of Mrs. Martin's." Matron was chattering on again. "It is lovely, isn't it? One of the nicest in the town, I think. I don't blame you for not wanting to live in here. Mind you, if ever you want to, there's a room here for you, you know. Now – " she slid off the table. "We must go and meet Doctor Foreman." She headed busily for the door. "Thank you for the coffee, Mrs. Newsome. And that lunch smells very good. What was the beef like? I told the butcher what I thought of the last lot – " She turned confidentially to Barbara. "I'm as much a housekeeper as a Matron here," she said. "All the food, all the stores – I buy the lot. It's a headache, I can tell you. But you'll soon learn all the ropes."

They found Doctor Foreman in the little Casualty Department, kneeling on the floor beside an old man, who sat with one foot in a bowl of warm water.

"Hello, m'dear," Doctor Foreman greeted Matron cheerfully, looking up at her through the tousled hair that fell on to his forehead. "Silly old Joe here got his bandage wet, let it dry on him, and now it's stuck to his ulcer. Isn't he daft?"

He was a very young, newly qualified doctor. Barbara thought, "About twenty-four, I suppose – more than five years younger than I am," and she smiled a little at the maternal way she looked at the young man on his knees beside his patient.

"Doctor Foreman's our only resident, Sister," Matron said. "And this is Sister Hughes, from the Royal, Doctor, so you'll have to mind your P's and Q's now. No flirting with my little cadets, or sister'll be after you."

He grinned up at Barbara with frank admiration. "I'm more likely to try to flirt with Sister," he said wickedly, and the old man in the chair chuckled evilly.

"And put my nose out of joint," Matron said equably.

"Ah well, I'm an old woman, I suppose – can't expect anything else."

"You'll do for me, Matron," the patient said unexpectedly, and put out a gnarled old hand to pinch Matron's ample bottom.

"And *you're* a naughty old man, Joe." She slapped his hand and turned to smile at Barbara. "Ten years we've been treating this silly old whatsit's varicose ulcer, and damned if the thing'll get better. I think he'd miss it if it did, wouldn't you, Joe?"

The old man grinned again, and turned back to watch Mike Foreman delicately ease the sodden dressing away from his leg, croaking instructions at him as he worked.

Oh, decidedly an odd sort of place, Barbara thought as she made her way back to the Martin house that evening after duty. But a very nice one, for all that. And she was surprised to find how little she missed the Royal. "I haven't thought about the old place since I got here – or about Daniel – " But the thought of Daniel did sting a little, after all, she found, when she remembered him, almost in the way a person with a bad tooth experimentally explores it with his tongue. "It's horrid to part with old friends on bad terms – " she told herself as she pushed open the door of the house. "That's why it bothers me – "

Geoffrey was standing, unexpectedly, in the hall as she came in pulling off her uniform gabardine coat.

"Geoffrey!" she said, surprise in her voice. "You're home early?"

He smiled at her, diffidently. "Well, there's this party tonight – "

"Party?" Barbara felt herself stiffen. "What party?"

48

"Mary's usual Monday affair. Didn't you know?"

Barbara shook her head, and started across the hall towards the stairs. "No," she said crisply over her shoulder. "I didn't. I hope you enjoy it."

"Barbara – " He put out a hand to stop her. "I know you were annoyed about that tea party Mary arranged and didn't tell you about – but she doesn't mean to upset you, you know – it's just – well, she's a bit of a bulldozer. But believe me, she means well – "

"That's damning with faint praise, isn't it?" Barbara said crossly. "And in any case – "

"Barbara, please – will you come to this party this evening? I usually find them a bit boring, to tell the truth, and I'm sure if you're there, it won't be," Geoffrey interrupted. "Please?"

She stood irresolutely at the foot of the stairs, looking down into his anxious, tired face, and then she smiled, ashamed of her bad temper. "Thank you – of course I will. And I'm sorry if I get cross with Mary. I know she really doesn't mean to upset people – and I daresay I'm a bit edgy, one way and another. What time?"

His face lit up. "Bless you, my dear. The first guests'll be here in – " he looked at his watch. "Oh, an hour or so. Time for a bath and a change for you, and perhaps a drink for the three of us before the mêlée begins. What say you?"

"See you in three quarters of an hour then," Barbara said, and went on her way upstairs. "After all," she told herself defiantly, as she wallowed in her hot bath, admiring the gleaming tiles and sparkling chrome fittings around her, "a party is a party. And if I know Mary, it will be a beautifully run one. I'm going to enjoy it. I *am* going to enjoy it!"

49

Chapter Four

The drawing-room looked delightful when Barbara came down. The big french windows were open on to the wide flagged terrace, and bowls of spring flowers starred the low tables. Mary had an eye for colour. All the flowers were yellow ones – daffodils and mimosa – and they gleamed against the purple upholstery and pale wood very attractively. Geoffrey was in a corner of the room, manipulating bottles and glasses. He turned and smiled at her as she came in.

"You look very nice," he said, a little diffidently. "Clever of you to wear yellow – it's the best colour for this room. You look like the daffodils."

Barbara felt shy suddenly. She was quite mature enough to accept a compliment gracefully, but a compliment from Geoffrey seemed odd, somehow.

"A rather wilted one, I'm afraid," she said awkwardly, smoothing her immaculate dark head with a gauche, childish gesture.

"Not at all! Now, what will you drink? Gin, whisky, sherry?"

"May I have something long and icy, please? Gin and lemonade perhaps?"

"A Tom Collins it is, then," and Geoffrey started

to mix her drink with expertise, clinking ice in a tall frosted glass.

They took their glasses across to the windows, and went out on to the terrace. There was a faint smell of newly cut grass in the air, mixing with the breath of the sea that was always present. Geoffrey sighed sharply, as he leaned on the low brick wall between the terrace and the lawn, and grinned a little ruefully over his shoulder at Barbara.

"This is the best part of these Monday parties for me," he said. "Once the guests arrive, the whole thing's a bore. But this is pleasant and quiet – restful."

"Why have parties if you don't like them?" Barbara came and rested her own arms on the wall beside him.

"Good policy parties, these," he said. "I meet clients and make new contacts. Mary's done a lot to build my practice up to what it is. It's an unusual Monday when I don't get at least one new client."

"I suppose that matters, of course – "

"You're quite right, my dear. It shouldn't."

Barbara flushed. Why wasn't she able to hide her private thoughts better than this? "I'm sorry – I didn't mean – "

Geoffrey smiled. "I know just what you mean. I've already got a very good practice. Why break my neck to enlarge it? The more work I do, the more tax I pay, and the net profit is negligible. But Mary's got into the habit of Monday parties, and it would seem odd if we stopped them now. For most of the locals it's the highlight of the week. Does that sound – conceited?"

"No – I don't think so – " Barbara picked her words carefully. "I can well believe it. This is a lovely house, and you are hospitable people – it's only natural people

51

should like coming here. But it seems a pity you can't relax more, doesn't it? You've been working very hard for years, haven't you? You should be able to spend more time doing what you want to do, instead of having to do what you think you ought to do."

Geoffrey looked at her sharply. "That's odd – "

"Odd?"

"You've said what I've been thinking myself – almost in the same words I'd use, if I ever used words to express a thought so – revolutionary."

Barbara stirred impatiently. "I just don't see it," she said. "Why shouldn't you do as you want to do sometimes? What stops you?"

His eyes slid away. "Oh, I don't know – the children – Mary – Your glass is empty. Have another drink." He took her glass from her, almost roughly, and went back to the table in the corner, bending his neat narrow shoulders over it so that his face was hidden from Barbara.

She watched him, puzzled. Obviously, she had said something that worried him, but quite what she wasn't sure. She felt obscurely embarrassed for a moment, as though for a brief moment she had glimpsed something she shouldn't have seen, as though she had walked in on somebody in their bath, and seen them exposed and stripped of the veneer they showed to the world. But when Geoffrey came back with her glass, he was himself again. Quiet, a little vague, rather colourless.

"This is a stiff one," he said. "It'll help you face the élite of Sandleas – and they take some facing, believe me," and his face crinkled into a smile. "Forgive me if I sounded a little depressed before. It's been a long day."

Barbara didn't have to answer. Mary swept into the room, looking magnificent in severely-cut black, her eyes separated by the deep line that appeared whenever she was annoyed.

"That idiot of a Lester woman forgot to put the prawns in the refrigerator, and they're uneatable now. We'll have to manage with just the anchovies – really, I sometimes wonder if anyone in this household is capable of doing anything without constant supervision. Geoffrey – did you remember to see Peter Blake about this evening?"

"Peter Blake?" Geoffrey closed his eyes for a moment. "Who? – oh yes – yes, he'll be here. Why did you particularly want him tonight? He's the dreariest man – "

"You can hardly call a man who owns and administers as much property as he does, dreary," Mary said tartly. "He's just – quiet. Lonely people often are."

Barbara stiffened. She didn't need telling that this Peter Blake had been invited for her benefit. Obviously rich and lonely meant, to Mary, unmarried. One of the eligibles, Barbara thought grimly. Mary *was* like a bulldozer. No matter what Barbara said to her about the subject, she was clearly determined to "get her sister settled". Barbara swallowed the rest of her drink at one gulp, ignoring the way her head spun a little from the alcohol. "We'll see," she thought grimly. "If Mary won't listen to me, I'll have to show her."

From the hall the sounds of arrival brought Mary's head up sharply, and with a last glance round the perfect room, she swept out.

Her voice drifted back from the hall. "My dear! So

nice to see you! How are the children? – Ah, Mr. Luton – so glad you could come – "

People began to drift into the room. Smooth, well dressed, elegant, the women looking as though they had been turned out of a beauty salon a few moments before, the men black-suited, red-faced, heads varnished to a smooth uniformity. Barbara murmured polite responses to Mary's introductions, shaking hands automatically, nodding politely at one face after another.

Within half an hour the room was full. The women's voices rose in a shrill cacophony of sound, the men rumbled an obbligato in the bass, and snatches of the conversation beat against Barbara's ears like waves on a beach. Mary moved sleekly from one person to another, breaking up groups that had been together for more than a few minutes, moving people from one part of the room to another as though they were chessmen on a board. Barbara, reckless, took another drink from the tray a white-aproned Mrs. Lester brought to her, and nibbled a sandwich a little guiltily. She ought to remember her ulcer –

"Barbara darling!" Mary's voice behind her pulled her round. "May I present a very old friend of mine? Peter Blake, my sister, Barbara Hughes."

He was a short man – a little shorter than Barbara, with sparse reddish hair pulled across a balding head. His eyes were a little bulbous – like a fish, Barbara thought with a giggle rising to her lips.

"Ah – yes – ah, how de do? Good party, what? Marvellous hostess, your sister – "

"Marvellous!" Barbara cried, watching Mary drift back across the room. "Isn't she just? Everything so

54

well organised – single people carefully introduced to each other – so tidy, isn't it?"

He blushed a brick red, then laughed uncertainly.

"Oh – yes – very funny – Ha ha! Yes – good joke that – " He threw back his head and laughed loudly, displaying his teeth. "Nothing like a sense of humour, is there? Keeps the old wheels turning – "

Barbara felt a little sick. To have been so abominably rude and then to be treated as though she had produced a gem of wit was dreadful. Across the room, Mary looked approvingly at her, obviously delighted to see her quiet spinster sister making such a hit. Barbara turned away, and saw Geoffrey behind her, being talked at by a fat man with a broad expanse of waistcoat winking with a gold chain.

Almost without thinking, she linked her arm into his, and smiled brilliantly at him. "Geoffrey darling," she said, her voice high and unnatural. "Mr. Blake thinks I have a sense of humour. Do you agree?" The fat man, at the sound of the word humour, clearly thought he should laugh, and did so, and Peter Blake, his green eyes blinking a little worriedly, dutifully followed suit. Barbara looked at Geoffrey again, and at the sight of his puzzled face, burst into a trill of laughter herself. And there they stood, laughing helplessly, even Geoffrey joining in, none of them having the least idea of what they were supposed to be laughing at.

Whether it was the drink, or the over-heated atmosphere, or her own reckless mood, Barbara was never quite sure, but for the next hour, she sparkled and scintillated like an accomplished society wit. More of Mary's guests joined the four people in the corner, and they became the focal point of the room. And all the time, even as she told them somewhat apocryphal stories of hospital happenings, all of them hilariously funny, some of them rather dubious, Barbara directed most of her sparkle at Geoffrey. She never let go of his arm, pointedly ignoring the pathetic Peter Blake, who seemed lost and bewildered as most of her jokes went over his head. She positively flirted with her brother-in-law.

The absurd thing, part of Barbara's mind noticed bleakly, was that her manoeuvres were having the diametrically opposite effect to the one she wanted. Peter Blake, instead of disappearing, disgusted by her behaviour, remained glued to her side, his mouth a little open, his eyes, admiring and glistening, never leaving her face. Mary, instead of being angry, didn't even notice that Barbara was flirting with her husband. She just preened and smiled constantly, patently delighted by what she considered her sister's good sense, by her "success". And Geoffrey – Geoffrey blossomed. He talked more than Barbara had ever heard him talk in a crowd, making wry acid comments that Barbara, in her heightened state of elation, found exquisitely funny. And each time she laughed at one of his sallies, Geoffrey seemed to open out more, to relax and become a stronger, more vivid person. Barbara drank no more, and as the effect of the three drinks she had taken began to wear off, she noticed, almost with alarm, that Geoffrey was drinking almost constantly.

What he drank seemed to have little effect on him, in the way drink is supposed to affect people. That is, he didn't become stupid, or over hilarious. His speech became more clear, his eyes sparkled, his laughter remained within bounds. But he responded to Barbara's provocative glances with a firmer hold on the arm she had linked into his. He began to play up to her, capping her jokes with more, leading her along so that she was able to sparkle more than ever. They behaved like two people delighted with each other.

It was nearly eleven when Barbara, with a murmured excuse, managed to extricate herself from the centre of the group, and made her way across the room to the hall. She stood there for a second, in the blessedly cool dimness, and pressed her hands to her aching head. She had hardly realised that her head *did* ache.

She dropped her hands to the back of her neck and flexed her shoulders a little. As she looked back into the brightly lit drawing-room, she had a sudden revulsion of feeling.

"How could I have behaved so abominably?" she thought drearily. "It was a revolting display – "

"Auntie Bar." The whisper that drifted from the staircase brought her round sharply. She peered into the darkness of the staircase, and as her eyes became more accustomed to the gloom, she could see Josie sitting curled up at the bend of the staircase, her fair hair drooping over her face, her dressing-gown pulled tightly round her thin shoulders.

"Josie! What on earth?"

"I've been watching the party," Josie said softly. "I usually do. Mrs. Lester gives me sandwiches and things. Are you enjoying yourself?"

Barbara climbed the stairs and slid down beside the child putting an arm across her bony little back.

"Oh, I suppose so," she said lightly. "That's what parties are for, aren't they?"

57

"Daddy doesn't usually like them." Josie turned her head and stared through the banisters to the brilliant patch that was the drawing room doorway. "But he's liking this one. I've been watching you."

Barbara suddenly went hot with shame. The thought of this sensitive child watching her display of girlish flirtation sickened her – and that her favourite aunt had been flirting with her father must have upset the child.

"Josie," she began awkwardly, but Josie snuggled her head against her aunt's shoulder and went on dreamily, "I'm ever so glad he likes this party, Auntie Bar. He doesn't like many things really, so it makes a nice change for him. You are nice to help him like it, Auntie Bar."

Barbara looked across the fair head to stare down into the room below. There was something infinitely pathetic about Josie, with her odd mixture of childish incomprehension, and almost motherly concern for her father's welfare. For a moment, Barbara remembered the way Josie had burst out with her dislike of her mother, and she felt sick again. The adults in this child's life seemed to make life dreadfully complicated.

But now Barbara was too tired, too confused to think much about anything. "Josie," she said gently. "You must go to bed, love. It's awfully late, and it's school tomorrow – "

"Oh, not yet, Auntie Bar! Please. Let me see them going home. They all look so funny, the way they nod away at each other, and they always say the same things – please, Auntie Bar!"

Before Barbara could answer, Mary came out into the hall below. "Barbara?" she called.

Josie slid back into the shadows, seeming to shrink into something too tiny to be seen. Barbara, after a moment, stood up and walked sedately down the stairs, as though she had come from the top. It would be too cruel to expose Josie to her mother's wrath.

"Yes?" she said coolly, as she reached the bottom. "Did you want me?"

"Not me, darling," Mary was bubbling, "everybody else does. You've made a tremendous hit, my dear. You've been hiding your light under a bushel all these years. Come along!"

Barbara grimaced a little at the cliché, but obediently followed her sister into the drawing-room, with a last look back at the drift of deeper shadow on the stairs that was Josie.

But, somewhat to Mary's chagrin, the party had begun to break up. People were drifting towards the door, murmuring platitudes, collecting handbags and dropped handkerchiefs and cigarette cases. The lights in the hall snapped on, and the guests began to shrug themselves into coats. Barbara looked sharply up the stairs, but the bend where Josie had sat, while still in the shadow, seemed empty.

She shook hands in farewell, smiled at the people who said consciously charming things about her, helped others find their scattered belongings. Peter Blake was almost the last to go, and he held on to her hand, his palm a little damp, as he said goodbye.

"Marvellous party, wasn't it – so tidy – " and he laughed loudly again at what he thought was Barbara's exquisitely funny joke. She managed to smile, and with a deft turn became involved in saying goobye to the few remaining people. Out of the corner of her eye, she could see Peter Blake going slowly and disconsolately through the front door, and managed to avoid looking at him. It was Geoffrey who came, a little unexpectedly, to her aid. He firmly escorted the last guest to the door, swept him and Peter Blake on the way to the cars, and left Barbara standing quietly in the hall.

Beside her, Mary sighed happily. "One of the best Mondays ever," she said contentedly. "You really are naughty, Barbara! To listen to you, anyone would be entitled to think you were the complete mouse! We must have more parties – " and she nodded happily, looking as contented as the cat who had stolen the cream.

Barbara was too tired to say a word. Tomorrow, she thought, I'll explain. Tomorrow.

"I'm going straight up, Barbara. You needn't wait, my dear. Geoffrey will lock up – Goodnight."

"Goodnight!" Barbara echoed, and watched her sister climb the stairs. Josie must have gone to bed, she thought. Mary walked past the bend in the stairs without a glance, and she must surely have seen the child had she been there, wide though the staircase was.

Geoffrey came back through the open front door, and closed it sharply behind him. He stood there for a second, and then he smiled at Barbara.

"Sister-in-law," he said gaily. "Sister-in-law, you are a positive angel."

He was still flushed and bright-eyed, cheerful from the drinks he had had. "I told you you'd make this party bearable, for me, didn't I? And you did more – you made it real pleasure. Come and have a drink!"

Barbara shook her head, and started to walk to the stairs. "No thank you, Geoffrey," she said. "I'm glad

60

you enjoyed yourself, but I'm so tired I could sleep on my feet. And I'm on duty at eight in the morning – "

"Oh, so what?" He followed her, and pulled her back beside him. "I insist – if it's only soda water. Come along." He led her back into the drawing-room. Barbara, genuinely tired, too tired to argue with him, sank into a chair.

"Oh, all right then," she said wearily. "Soda water, and that's all – " and she closed her eyes against the bright lights that made her head ache more.

And then, suddenly, she felt strong hands grasping her elbows and she was pulled to her feet. She opened her eyes sharply, and stared at Geoffrey's face suddenly so close to hers.

"Geoffrey! What in hell? – " But she could say no more. His arms were round her, and he buried his face in her shoulder, murmuring something she couldn't hear. She tried to push him away, but he was too strong for her, kissing her neck, seeking her face, as she twisted and turned in an attempt to escape.

"Geoffrey – you – stop it – " But with one firm hand he took her chin, and pulled her face round to meet his. For a fraction of a second he stared at her, and then his mouth was on hers, burning hot, urgent, almost bruising her mouth in the intensity of his kiss.

She struggled violently, but it was as though she were a kitten, so little effect did her attempts have. He went on, murmuring thickly, kissing her again and again. And then she managed to get an arm free, and brought it back sharply to deliver a stinging blow on to the side of his face.

There was absolute silence for a second. Then he dropped his arms and stood, rigid and absolutely still, staring at her, his face chalk white except for the flaming marks Barbara's fingers had left.

"Oh my God," he said, almost in a whisper, taking a deep shuddering breath. "I must be – Barbara – " He put a hand out towards her, almost beseechingly, but she pulled away from him, to stand, still and angry, looking at him, her mouth twisted in disgust.

"You're drunk – " Her voice was icy. "Revoltingly drunk – "

He shook his head, muzzily, as though to clear it. "Yes – I must be – " He rubbed his head with a suddenly shaking hand. "Please forgive me – Barbara, please. I beg your pardon. I don't know what came over me." He looked at her helplessly for a moment, the sparkle and personality that had invested him during the party quite gone, his old drab self again. "You looked rather like Mary for a moment – the Mary I first knew. You are both – beautiful – I'm sorry."

Barbara, rubbing her forehead wearily, felt suddenly deflated. Her rage and disgust evaporated almost as fast as they had come. "Forget it," she said dully, "it was as much my fault, I suppose. I've been behaving like a – like a tart all evening – Oh yes I have," she rode over his protests. "And you have drunk too much. Forget it. I'm going to bed."

She turned and went to the door, and then she stopped. "I'll arrange to move into the Nurses' Home tomorrow," she said, her back to him. "I don't think I should stay here, after all."

There was silence for a second. Then Geoffrey said, evenly, "I think perhaps you are right. It might be better all round. Goodnight, Barbara. And please forgive me." She nodded, wearily, and still without turning, went out and on up the stairs. As she went into her room she thought she heard a door close softly across the corridor. She turned her head to look, but all the doors were closed, Jamie's, Josie's, the spare bedroom, their blank whiteness gleaming at her in the dim light.

She pulled her clothes off and dropped them haphazardly on the floor, something she had never done in her life before. And after a moment's thought, she took a small bottle from a box in her bedside cabinet, and swallowed one of the bright red capsules it contained. She needed to sleep tonight, more than she needed anything. And without help, that would be impossible.

Chapter Five

"I'm sorry, Mary," Barbara said again, trying not to sound mulish. "I just think it would be better for all of us if I lived at the hospital. And anyway, there might well be times when I shall have to be on call at night – when Matron's away. You won't want the house disturbed by the 'phone ringing in the middle of the night – "

"That is absolute nonsense," Mary snapped, "and you know it. By all means sleep at the hospital on nights you must be on call but there is no reason at all for you to live anywhere but here while you are in Sandleas. You are just being stupid and silly."

Barbara's mouth tightened. This discussion had been going on for nearly a quarter of an hour now, and how she had kept her temper she didn't know. She had tried everything she knew to persuade Mary that living in hospital would be the best thing for her to do – everything, that is, except the truth. Now, for a wild moment, she almost blurted out the truth. "I can't stay here any longer because your husband kissed me last night, and neither he nor I want to live in the same house any longer." But how could she? Particularly as Barbara still felt a sick shame when she remembered the way she had used Geoffrey as someone to flirt with. So she tried again.

"Mary," she said with all the patience she could muster, "I'm not used to living in an ordinary house. I've lived in a nurses' home for the past ten years. I'm just more – well, more at home living in hospital – "

"Then it's time you made an effort to learn how to live in an ordinary house. Shutting yourself up like that won't get you anywhere."

This time Barbara's control snapped. She stood up from the breakfast table where she and Mary were sitting, and resting both hands on it, she stared at her sister with naked dislike on her pale face.

"I've told you till I'm hoarse that I don't want to be *settled*, as you so elegantly put it. I'm not here to be trotted round and shown to various men until one of them takes me off the marriage market. Do you understand? I know exactly what you mean by 'not getting anywhere' but I'm quite happy as I am. Just because you have a mind that doesn't go beyond running your house and bullying your husband and children and anyone else you can find to bully, you think that's the only way to live. Well it isn't the way I want to live, thank you. I'm a nurse, and I like being a nurse. If I marry it will be incidental – not just something that's convenient, and comfortable, but something that happens by itself." Barbara stopped, trembling a little, and stared at her sister's rigid white face. For a brief moment she wanted to stop, to make an effort to re-establish the uneasy relationship they used to have. But it was too late for that.

"You make me sick," she said, her voice, usually so low and quiet, pitched to an almost hysterical shrillness. "You see the world as something that exists just for your convenience. People are something you push around

65

as though they were – were pawns on a chessboard. You've made your daughter into a frightened neurotic child, your husband is a pale carbon copy of the man he ought to be – thank God your son's got enough strength to keep his mind to himself. Well, I'm a bit like him, I hope. I've got a mind of my own, and I'll run my own life. I'm damned if I'll let you decide what I shall do, and where I live – I'll see you in hell first! I'm moving out of this house, and I never want to see you again as long as I live – " and she threw her napkin, still clutched in her cold hand, on to the table in front of her, and ran, almost blindly, from the dining-room.

She slammed the door behind her, and stood shaking and sick in the hall outside, her eyes closed as she tried to regain her calm.

After a second she opened them – and saw Josie standing very quietly in front of her.

"Josie – " she said after a moment, "I thought you'd gone to school – "

"I forgot my algebra book." The child didn't look at her, keeping her head bent as she fumbled in the satchel slung over her shoulder. "I had to come back for it – "

"Oh, I see – " Barbara tried to make her voice sound normal and relaxed. "Have you only just come back, or – ?" Had Josie heard her shouting so bitterly at Mary? After the emotional storm Josie had had, when she had said that she hated her mother, the last thing Barbara wanted was to let the child realise that her aunt, too, felt the same way.

But Josie merely said "Mmm?" and brushed past her into the drawing-room, looking vaguely about her for the missing book. After a second or two she came back, and still not looking at her aunt, said, "I must have left it at

66

school – I'd better go. I'll be late. 'Bye Auntie Bar – "
and she ran towards the hall door.

"Jo – " Barbara ran after her. "Look Josie, I'm afraid
I won't be here when you get back today – I'm going to
live in the hospital. It might be easier if I do – " she said
lamely.

Josie stopped, and without turning, said, "Oh –
are you?"

"I have to be on call at night, you see, sometimes, so I
have to be there. Perhaps – perhaps you'd care to come
there to tea with me one afternoon?"

There was a moment of silence. Then Josie said,
"Yes – that would be nice. I must go, I'll be late –
'Bye Auntie Bar."

Barbara watched her as she ran off down the drive,
her heavy satchel thumping against her legs as she
ran.

"Josie must have heard," she thought dully. "Poor
Josie. Whatever I do it seems to be the wrong thing.
I'll meet her after school one afternoon – perhaps I'll
be able to explain – "

Then, squaring her shoulders, she turned and went
into Geoffrey's study.

As she dialled the number of the hospital on the
telephone, she heard the rattle of brooms and buckets
in the hall outside as Mrs. Lester started the day's work.
Then Matron's voice was clacking tinnily at her from the
telephone.

Succinctly she explained that she had, after all,
decided to take a room in the Nurses' Home. Would
Matron mind if she arrived late for duty this morning,
and brought her luggage with her?

"My dear, by all means! It will be nice to have you here

– but won't you miss that lovely house? We aren't nearly so comfortable here, I'm afraid – "

"Not at all," Barbara said crisply, "I'm used to nurses' homes. I'll be there as soon as I can make it, Matron."

Whether it was because Mary had planned it that way, or by accident, Barbara didn't know, but she saw no one as she hurried up the wide staircase to her room. She packed her cases with the speed and method that had been developed during the years of the rigid discipline of nursing, and, with her head high walked out of the pretty blue room, and down the stairs. She could hear the whine of Mrs. Lester's vacuum cleaner above the sound of "Housewives' Choice" on the kitchen radio, but that was all. Mary's voice, usually raised loudly as she gave the day's instructions to Mrs. Lester, or arranged one of her countless committee meetings on the telephone, was silent.

Barbara wondered if she should go and look for her sister to say goodbye. "After all," she told herself, "it's common courtesy to say goodbye when one leaves someone's house – " but she didn't. Whatever efforts Barbara made, the sisters were parting in acrimony. Seeking Mary now might merely lead to more bitter words, more anger. Better to leave things alone, bad as they were.

So, humping her two suitcases herself, Barbara walked out of the big comfortable house and down the well-kept drive. And even though she still felt upset by the argument, still ashamed of her behaviour at the previous evening's party, still embarrassed by Geoffrey's unexpected amorousness after the party, her main sensation was one of overriding relief. She was going back to where she belonged – to live in hospital.

Chapter Six

The next two weeks slid by quickly for Barbara. She liked her shabby little bed-sitting-room on the second floor of the hospital. It wasn't as pretty as her room at Mary's house had been, admittedly. The wardrobe was scratched and old, the drawers of the dressing table stuck each time she tried to open one, the bed creaked a little, the carpet was thin and dingy. But it was what she was used to, she told herself – it felt homely and comfortable. If she sometimes did miss the organised rich comfort of Mary's house, sometimes regretted the good food that appeared on Mary's table when she faced hospital stew and prunes for lunch, she managed to stifle her yearnings after comfort.

But even when she busied herself about her work in the little hospital, she couldn't help wondering about the family she had left behind. What had Jamie thought when he found his aunt had gone? Try as she might, she couldn't possibly imagine what his reaction had been. He was such a self-contained boy, so silent, living his life in a sort of cocoon of preoccupation with his own affairs. And Josie? What of her?

"Surely she must miss me?" Barbara thought a little unhappily. The child had spent so much time with her aunt, had shown her affection so nakedly. Barbara half expected to see her at any time, half hoped that she would come to the hospital one afternoon on her way home after school to have the tea Barbara had promised. But she didn't, and Barbara decided to wait a little while before seeking her niece out, and trying to re-establish the old relationship. She felt obscurely that the frightened, shy Josie needed her, that she had almost a duty to look after her. "But I mustn't try to rush her," she told herself. "Children need time – "

As for Geoffrey – she thought of him as little as possible. But sometimes, almost against her will, she found his face appearing in her mind's eye, the face that was usually so closed and expressionless. But when she did think of him, she saw him not as he usually was, but as he had looked the night of the party, his eyes glittering with amusement, his usually pale face flushed. Often, as she fell asleep at night she would find herself remembering the way he had held her, had kissed her with such rough passion, the passion that she knew he had meant for her, even though he had said he had kissed her because she reminded him of the young Mary.

Barbara was not a stupid woman. Had the episode really been the result of too much drink and her resemblance to Mary, she knew quite well that she would have been able to ignore it – to treat it as a rather foolish piece of bad behaviour that didn't matter. She knew, too, that Geoffrey realised there was more to the matter than that. She could hear his voice again as he had said in reply to her announcement that she would leave the house, "I think perhaps you are right. It would be better all round – " Geoffrey too recognised the attraction he felt for her for what it was. A real and potentially powerful thing that could, if unchecked, develop into something much stronger than it had any right to be.

Barbara would stir restlessly as she tried to ignore the thoughts that rose, unbidden, to her mind. The whole situation was so explosive. The dislike she felt for her sister meant that propinquity had turned into real hate – the way Josie had said she preferred her aunt to her mother, the way Barbara, try as she might to deny it to herself, liked – indeed revelled in – the comfort and richness of Mary's home. It would have been the easiest thing in the world to make use of Geoffrey's attraction for her.

Sometimes her thoughts would develop into actual fantasy. She found herself imagining life married to Geoffrey, mothering the two children, running the house –

When this happened Barbara would rouse herself from her half-sleep and thump her pillow in anger at herself.

"If I had fallen in love with Geoffrey it wouldn't be so wicked, somehow," she told herself honestly. "But I don't care for him like that. I'm sorry for him – I like him – he's a comfortable person to be with, but that's all – " and she would take a sleeping pill in an effort to sleep quickly, so that her mind couldn't play these tricks on her, making her imagine things she had no right to imagine.

Matron Elliott, with unexpected tact, said nothing at all about Barbara's decision to live at the hospital. She just went on her usual garrulous way, running her hospital with a casual efficiency that kept staff and patients happy. And Barbara threw herself into learning all she could about the running of the place, burying herself in the best therapy she knew – work.

Her days were so full and happy that she found herself loth to go off duty at night. She would almost make work for herself, going round the little wards, teaching the assistant nurses and cadets all she could. She would spend long hours in the little operating theatre, polishing the instruments that were so rarely needed, cleaning the tiled walls and re-arranging the cupboards of equipment.

She came to know the patients very well, too. There was a delightful old man in the corner bed of the tiny men's ward who was almost a fixture of the place, he had been there so long. He had diabetes, and both his legs had been amputated years before.

He would sit up in his bed, watching all that happened about him with beady eyes, telling all the nurses exactly what to do and how to do it, bossing the other patients about so cheerfully that they loved him for it.

Barbara would find the old man surrounded by half the other patients in the ward as they played noisy games of pontoon, and learned to smile sympathetically and ignore the coins scattered on the counterpane, even though in her own Royal Hospital patients had never been allowed to gamble. She accepted that this Cottage Hospital was nothing like the Royal – that patients behaved more like privileged guests than ill people who were there to be treated and discharged as soon as possible.

In the women's ward the patients would congregate in the little kitchen in the evenings, even the ones in wheelchairs crushing themselves in, to gossip and giggle over strong sweet tea. And Barbara would remember the way she had been trained never to give patients stimulating drinks at night, yet still would join them in their sessions most evenings.

She remembered, too, the way the Matron of the Royal had said that she had learned more about people during her days in a cottage hospital than she had learned in all her years at the Royal, and smiled a little at the memory. Matron had been quite right, Barbara would think, sitting perched on the kitchen table among the patients, listening to them talk. There had never been time for this at the Royal – and what a pity it was. On those evenings Barbara really heard what it was like to live the life of a woman in a small cottage, heard how they had struggled to bring up broods of children in cramped homes, with husbands often out of work, with hungry mouths to be fed on a few pence a meal. She would watch their worn fingers working on knitting for grandchildren, listen to their sometimes ribald comments on the people they knew, and marvel at their calm good humour in the face of fear and danger.

Like Mrs. Innes, who had a cancer that she knew would kill her – that would kill her soon. But she would grin cheerfully at Barbara when the breathlessness that was the result of her disease attacked her, saying "Gawd 'elp us, Sister – you'd think there was enough air to go round, wouldn't you? Must be all these others breathing too much what does it. They don't leave enough for me – " and the other women would tease her, and with rough sympathy push her back to her bed, helping her out of her wheelchair while Barbara and the little nurse on duty went to prepare an injection and inhalation to give the temporary relief that was all that could be offered the dying woman.

It was a week after Barbara had come to live in the

hospital that she was called out late one night to Mrs. Innes. Matron was away for the weekend so Barbara was on call, and she scrambled into her uniform and hurried down to the ward, a little frightened as she always was at the thought of having to see a very ill patient. Even after ten years of nursing, the sight of pain and fear in a patient upset her. That had been why she had preferred to work in the operating theatres.

The ward was dim and silent as she came into it that night. None of the other women moved, but Barbara knew they were awake. Somehow, it is always possible to know whether the patients in the ward are waking or sleeping, even if they lie still with their eyes closed. Tonight, they were all awake, the ward full of that somehow electric atmosphere that seemed to come by itself whenever a patient was dying.

Behind the screens in the corner a light burned dimly, and Barbara could hear the rough breathing of the woman behind it. She slipped round the screens and stood there for a second, watching. Doctor Foreman was leaning over the bed, his eyes blank as he concentrated on listening to the rattle that filled his ears from the stethoscope pressed against Mrs. Innes' bulky chest. The little assistant nurse stood beside him, frightened and looking as though she felt sick.

Mike Foreman looked up after a moment, and grimaced at Barbara, turning his mouth down in a gesture of finality as he looked back at Mrs. Innes' closed eyes and pale face.

"I doubt if she'll last till morning," he whispered. "I've looked at the notes, and her only relative is a son in New Zealand – nothing more we can do."

Barbara nodded, and moved over to stand beside the high white bed. Doctor Foreman scribbled something on the chart that hung at the foot of the bed, and then, with a nod at Barbara, slipped out of the little pool of light the screens enclosed.

"No point in my staying, I'm afraid," he murmured. "I'll be upstairs if you want me," and he was gone. Barbara didn't blame him. No one wanted to stay with a dying patient if they could help it.

The little assistant nurse stirred uneasily. Barbara smiled at her. 'Go and make tea for the patients who are awake," she said softly. "Most of them are, I think. Have some yourself."

The nurse smiled gratefully, and hurried silently away. The tea, Barbara thought, looking down on the patient beside her, wouldn't hurt the patients and would give the nurse something to do – and that was what she needed most right now.

She pulled a chair over, and sat down, smoothing her apron over her knees. Then she put her hand on to the white worn one lying on the counterpane, and just sat and watched the face on the pillow.

The ward rustled with soft movement as patients sat up and gratefully accepted the cups of tea the nurse brought. There was a faint tinkle of spoon on cup, the sounds of women rummaging in their lockers for the private stores of sweet biscuits. The sounds seemed to penetrate Mrs. Innes' consciousness, for she stirred a little, and then opened her eyes to stare at Barbara in puzzlement. The pale blue eyes, the irises ringed with white, considered her thoughtfully, and then Mrs. Innes smiled.

"Sister – " she murmured. Barbara leaned over her

and touched the worn cheek. "Yes," she said gently. "It's me. Do you want anything?"

Mrs. Innes frowned for a moment.

"Billy – " she whispered. "I'd like to see our Billy – "

"Who is Billy?" Barbara's voice was gentle.

The eyes opened again. "Billy? My boy. Such a boy he was – such a pretty boy – " She turned her head uneasily on the pillow.

"I keep tellin' 'im to keep away from there – " her voice dropped to an uneasy mutter, and for a while she seemed to ramble, her words coming in disjointed bursts, before sinking back into an incomprehensible murmur.

Barbara said nothing. She just held the hand on the counterpane more firmly, her finger on the fluttering uneven pulse, and watched the face in front of her.

Twenty minutes slid by, and Mrs. Innes seemed to have slipped back into her semi-comatose state. Then, suddenly, she opened her eyes and looked straight at Barbara.

"I'd like to see our Billy," she said clearly. "But it's too late now – all those years ago he went – and I daresay she's made a good enough wife for him after all. It wasn't worth a row, was it?"

"I daresay you're right," Barbara said, not quite sure what she could say. Clearly Mrs. Innes was remembering something that had happened years ago, but without knowing just what, there was little she could offer in the way of comfort. Mrs. Innes stared at her again, and repeated, "Not worth a row – " and then closed her eyes again.

Around her, Barbara felt rather than heard the ward settle down again after the tea. Mrs. Innes didn't speak again, and Barbara, watching her, realised that she had slipped now into a deep coma. As far as Mrs. Innes was concerned, the fears and the breathlessness were over. She wouldn't wake again. But Barbara sat on, listening to the stertorous breathing, checking the fragile pulse, automatically noting observations on the chart at the foot of the bed.

It must have been about one in the morning when the little assistant nurse appeared from behind the screens at Barbara's back.

"Sister – "

Barbara looked up, almost startled. She had somehow been alone in the world with this tired old woman she was watching.

"Yes, Nurse?"

The other looked frightened again, "Please, Sister, Doctor Foreman says you're to come at once. There's been some accident – the police have brought a lady in – casualty, he says. Can you come?"

Barbara looked down at Mrs. Innes. "Yes," she said. "Look, my dear. There's nothing to worry about here. You can't do anything to help Mrs. Innes, I'm afraid, and she's quite comfortable. You needn't sit with her any more, I don't think. Just check her pulse for me every half hour, and watch her. I doubt if she'll wake up again – she's very deeply unconscious – but I doubt if she'll die before morning. If you get at all worried, ask nurse from the babies' ward to come and fetch me, will you?"

The little nurse nodded, still frightened, but clearly relieved that she wouldn't have to sit and watch Mrs. Innes.

Barbara hurried silently to the babies' ward. The night nurse in there was an older woman, she remembered with relief. As Barbara put her head round the door, she couldn't help liking what she saw, even in the course of her hurry.

The night nurse was sitting in an armchair before the fire, sewing tapes on a pile of babies' bibs. The firelight leaped and glinted on the nursery pictures on the walls, glancing off the shining row of feeding bottles on the trolley, illuminating the flushed sleeping faces of the four children, on the starfish hands sprawled on pillows in the touching helplessness of sleep.

"Nurse," Barbara whispered hurriedly. "I must go to Casualty – some sort of accident, I gather – and Mrs. Innes is dying, I'm afraid. Could you help Nurse Foster, do you think, if you aren't too busy? She'd be glad of company."

"Of course, Sister." She glanced round at her four sleeping babies. 'These monkeys are out for the count. I'll prop the door open and stay with Foster – don't you fret."

Barbara hurried on her way down the darkened corridor towards the Casualty Department, marvelling again at the difference between this cottage hospital and the Royal. She couldn't imagine a Royal nurse being able to leave her ward to help another nurse – but then, she reminded herself, we had lots of nurses at the Royal.

She pushed the door of the Casualty room open, and stood blinking owlishly for a moment in the glare that assaulted her eyes after the dimness of the ward. Doctor Foreman and a policeman were standing in one corner in quiet talk, and the nurse from the private rooms was standing beside the high table in the middle of the room. There was a patient lying there, humped under a blanket that was stained ominously with blood. Barbara couldn't quite see the patient's face, so she moved silently round to stand beside the table.

Doctor Foreman looked up and saw her at the same moment and started forward, the policeman, too, looking up sharply. The nurse tried clumsily to hide the patient's face with her body, but it was too late.

For a moment they all stood frozen and stared at Barbara as she looked down at the face on the green mackintosh pillow. She could hear the loud ticking of the clock, the faint hiss of steam from the steriliser, the chugging of an ambulance engine in the yard outside, and as she stood there she felt a cold wave of horror spread over her body.

The face on the pillow was white, smeared with dirt and blood, blood that was running from a hideous wound in the forehead. And under the dirt and the blood Barbara recognised Mary's face.

Chapter Seven

For a long moment there was silence in the brilliantly lit Casualty room. Then Mike Foreman spoke, his voice unnaturally high and strained.

"My God – I'm sorry, Sister. We – we'd only just realised who she was – I didn't know when I sent for you – I was going to send nurse to stop you – "

Barbara stood still and silent, staring at Mary's face, the face that was so familiar, yet so strange in its still emptiness. Then she raised her head and looked at Mike.

"Stop me?" she said stupidly.

He came and stood beside her, putting his hand on her shoulder with clumsy sympathy.

"I wouldn't have had this happen for the world," he said miserably. "I'm – sorry."

She nodded dumbly, and looked again at Mary's face. Then, with an almost visible effort, she said, "What are you going to do? How – how bad is she?"

"I'm waiting for a radiologist to come from Dover with a portable machine – our's is on the blink. But I think she's got a fracture, I'm afraid. She's deeply unconscious – I've asked Josephs to come from Dover in case she needs a decompression – more than that, at the moment, we can't do – "

Barbara nodded again. Mary, with a fractured skull? Mary needing an operation?

"It's impossible!" she thought wildly. "Mary's much too efficient to let a thing like this happen – "

At the back of the room the policeman moved slightly, and Barbara looked up at him. "What happened?" she asked, her voice hoarse.

"It was the cliff road, Sister," he said, his voice thick with embarrassment. "Far as we can tell, she missed that right bend near the Crown, right at the top there, and hit the wall – how she didn't go right over was a miracle – "

"I see." Barbara's voice was low. "Does Geoffrey – have you told her husband?"

"We've only this minute found who she was – " The policeman held out Mary's smart handbag, looking incongruous in his big red hand. "Shall I 'phone now? or p'raps you'd rather – " His voice died away, and he looked at her helplessly, clearly bewildered by the turn events had taken.

Barbara shook her head decisively. "I think you had better call him," she said clearly. "I must stay here. There's work to do – "

"No!" Mike's protest was sharp. "My dear, you *can't* look after her yourself. I couldn't let you – it would be too unkind – "

"I'm the only trained nurse here," Barbara said levelly. "The nurses on duty are all cadets and untrained staff. And you can't manage on your own."

"Matron – "

" – is staying overnight in London. So that's that," Barbara said crisply. "Look, we'd better put her in that empty private room. The radiologist can take her films there, and it's next door to the theatre. I think we can move her on this table – unless you'd rather she stayed here?"

Mike pulled himself together. "No, you're right. She'll be better in a bed. I'll put up a plasma drip as soon as we get her settled. Josephs should get here soon – "

Almost like an automaton, Barbara set to work. Together she and Mike trundled the heavy Casualty table along the darkened corridors; together, they lifted Mary gently into the narrow white bed in the little single roon next to the operating theatre. And while Mike himself prepared the equipment for the intravenous infusion of plasma, the little nurse and Barbara gently undressed Mary, bathed the white face, and arranged the room.

Afterwards, when Barbara had sent the nurse to make a round of the other patients, and she stood alone in the room, looking down on her sister's still face, the white bandage hardly more white than the cheeks below it, she tried to collect her thoughts. This was Mary, she told herself. Mary, her own sister. But somehow, the rush of feeling she ought to experience just didn't come. She felt numb, and somehow no more involved than she would be if this patient were a complete stranger.

"But she's desperately ill," she told herself. "She might die – " but even this thought couldn't rouse her. Barbara rested her fingertips lightly on Mary's wrist, finding the uneven pulse, frighteningly rapid. "She's bleeding – " she thought. "And her unconsciousness is deepening. Intra-cranial haemorrhage – "

Behind her the door opened. The radiologist, a young woman whose eyes were still a little fogged with the sleep she had been woken from, trundled the big portable

82

X-ray machine into the room. Barbara stood back, and watched as the girl arranged the metal plate that contained the film under Mary's head, watched her set the apparatus, heard the buzz as the film was taken – and still felt nothing. No fear, nothing but a dumb acceptance. Since that first wave of horror had spread over her at the first sight of Mary, since it had gone, she had been like this. Quite unfeeling.

Mr. Josephs arrived as the girl took the film away to be developed. He nodded his grey head at Barbara, and with Mike close at his side, leaned over the bed.

There was silence as his long fingers removed the temporary dressing Barbara had put on, and gently touched the wound and felt the bone behind it. He listened to Mary's chest, took her blood-pressure and pulse, and then straightened up with a little grunt.

"Don't need an X-ray to confirm this," he said, his voice loud in the silent room. "Shattered like an egg shell. I'll try to clean it up, and get the splinters out, but it's a poor hope – she's bleeding fast – have you got any blood for her?"

"I'm just going to start some plasma, sir," Mike said nervously. "Then I'll cross match – but I thought I'd better get the drip going first. I was just about to start when you arrived – "

Mr. Josephs nodded. "Mmm. She'd be better off at Dover, of course, but I doubt if we'd get her there. Relatives informed? They'd better be warned – she won't do much – "

"Sir – " Mike interrupted, his face agonised with embarrassment. "Sister Hughes here – the patient is her sister – "

"Eh?" The surgeon looked up sharply at Barbara,

standing quietly beside the bed. "Good God – I say, I'm sorry, Sister! I'd no idea – you shouldn't be looking after her yourself, should you? Too much strain for you – she's so ill!" He turned to Mike, his face angry. "For Christ's sake man, what are you thinking of? Send for another nurse, will you, even if Sister is on duty here! You can't expect her to – "

"There isn't anyone else, sir." Barbara's voice cut across Mike's attempt to explain. "I'm the only trained nurse on duty tonight. And I'm quite able to cope, thank you. Please don't worry about me."

Josephs stared at her under his grey brows, and then nodded. "I see, my dear. Well, I'm sorrier than I can say about this, but I must warn you – she is extremely ill."

"I know, sir," Barbara said quietly. "I would be grateful if you would speak to my brother-in-law when he comes. I don't think I could manage that – "

"Of course, of course, my dear – " He touched Mary's pulse again. "Sister, I'd like to operate in as short a time as possible – can you – I mean can you – " he floundered.

"I was Theatre Sister at the Royal for some years, sir."

His relief was almost comical. "Were you, by George! Well, well! What are you doing in a cottage hospital then? – Beg pardon, m'dear. Impertinent of me – none of my business." And he almost blushed.

The little nurse from the private rooms slid nervously round the door. "Sister – " she whispered. "Mr. Martin is here – "

Mr. Josephs looked up sharply. "Your brother-in-law, m'dear? I'll see him now – " and he hurried from the room, his face settling again into his original stern lines.

"Nurse – " Rapidly, Barbara gave the little junior instructions. "Stay here with the patient, will you? Take her pulse every ten minutes, and chart it here. I'll set up the theatre, so I'll be right next door if you're at all worried. I won't be any longer than I can help. Doctor Foreman – "

Mike hurried round the bed to stand beside her, looking at her with almost ludicrous concern.

"Will you be good enough to manage this drip on your own? And when it's up, perhaps you'd go along and see Mrs. Innes for me – she's in coma, so there isn't much we can do. But I'd be glad if you'd look at her." Barbara made for the door, pulling her cuffs off as she went. "Sorry to leave you like this, but I'm the only one who can get the theatre ready – "

As she snapped the lights on in the tiny theatre, and hurried into the tight cap and mask and gown, she felt the first moment of fear for Mary. The surgeon clearly thought she would die.

But then, as she set about the familiar tasks of preparing the theatre, filling the sterilisers with bowls and dishes, getting out the instruments, laying out gloves and dressings, she reminded herself of the old Hippocratic maxim. "No head injury is so slight that it should be ignored, nor none so severe that life should be despaired of."

She was ready in half an hour. The theatre bustled into life. Mike and the nurse from the private rooms brought Mary in, and Barbara helped to lift her on to the table. Then, as Josephs and Mike scrubbed up, and the junior nurse stood by ready to tie them into their gowns, Barbara, her fingers moving delicately and smoothly, cut away the hair round the hideous gash on

85

Mary's forehead. As she clipped away the black hair, so like her own, except for the lines of white in it, she shivered a little. Mary couldn't possibly die, she assured herself. Not the efficient Mary.

By the time she had herself scrubbed up, and come to the table, smoothing the thin brown rubber of her gloves over her fingers, the men had towelled up. Across the theatre, the anaesthetist who had come from Dover with the surgeon frowned over the faintly moving respiration bag on the machine. Barbara noticed, almost automatically, that he was giving no anaesthetic, only oxygen. "She's too deeply out already," she thought. And then she turned her attention to the work before her.

Mr. Josephs, forceps held poised in one slim brown hand, peered at her over his mask.

"You're sure you can manage, Sister?" he asked gruffly. "It's a dreadful strain when the patient is an acquaintance, let alone a close relative – "

"I can manage, sir," Barbara said evenly. "Will you be needing burrs?"

His eyes creased in a tight smile. "Good girl," he said. "No burrs yet. Explore first," and he bent his head to the towelled shape in front of him.

The little room settled into an uneven quiet. Barbara could hear the faint hiss of the anaesthetic machine, the occasional clank as the anaesthetist knocked the oxygen cylinders, the click of instrument against instrument. The nurse hovered nervously in the background, her eyes strained and scared as she avoided looking at the area where the surgeon's fingers probed and explored.

"Poor little monkey – " Barbara thought, as she broke open the tubes of fine silk and catgut sutures. "I should have spent more time with her before, telling her what to do – she must be terrified – " but she couldn't spare more time to think about the nurse. Josephs was having trouble. She could see the fine beads of sweat forming on his wide forehead, the tight lines of strained concentration on his face, as he tried desperately to remove the splinters of bone that were embedded in the soft tissues of Mary's brain.

When it happened it was so sudden that Barbara had not time to think. A sudden spurt of vivid red blood stained the front of Josephs' gown just as the anaesthetist called out, his voice shrill with anxiety " – she's stopped breathing – can't find a pulse – "

Even as Josephs tried desperately to find and stop the tear in the bleeding artery, Mike pulled the sheet back from Mary's body, and with an outflung hand almost shouted at Barbara, "Knife – I'll try a heart massage – "

They worked desperately. Mike, with a skill Barbara would not have expected in so newly qualified a man, opened the chest, deftly, and with steady even movements, massaged the heart. For a moment, the blood pulsed feebly in the head wound, and then the pulsation stopped, settling down to a slow oozing that showed that the heart was no longer pumping blood round the still body on the table. Frantically, the anaesthetist pumped away at the respiration bag, in a vain effort to fill the lungs with oxygen.

But even as she worked, giving Josephs swabs and forceps, filling a syringe with a heart stimulant for Mike to inject direct into the heart muscle, she knew it was too late. Mary was dead. Dead.

Almost at the same moment, the three doctors faltered in their work, and stopped. They looked at each other, and then Josephs pulled his mask wearily away from his face, and looked at Barbara.

"I'm sorry, Sister," he said dully. "It was – almost inevitable," and he gently pulled the sheet back across the wound in Mary's forehead, covering her completely. Mike, without raising his head, pulled his gloves off and dropped them on the floor.

Josephs came round the table, and put his hand on Barbara's shoulder where she stood silent and still in her place.

"Come along, my dear," he said gently, and with a firm pressure led her out of the theatre into the ante-room beyond.

She stood there for a moment, swaying a little with fatigue. Without thinking about it, she noticed the clock on the wall in front of her, automatically noting the time of death for the record she would later have to make. Five-thirty. Was it so long since the little nurse had come to Mrs. Innes' bedside, and told her she was wanted in Casualty?

She could see the first lightening of the morning sky beyond the windows, heard the early stirrings of the hospital outside the door. It was morning, a spring morning, and Mary was dead.

She took a deep shuddering breath. Then, almost to her surprise, she heard her own voice:

"I must go to the ward. There is a patient there – "

"Never mind that." Josephs sounded brusque, the brusqueness of sympathy. "They'll have to manage without you – "

She shook her head. "I must go. Mrs. Innes – she's dying – "

He bit his lip, and then with an almost imperceptible

shrug, dropped his hand from her shoulder. "Yes – I daresay you're right. I'd want to work, too. I – I'll speak to your brother-in-law now."

The women's ward was rustling with movement, scattered pools of light showing over beds where patients had woken early. One of the patients on her way to the bathroom padded past Barbara where she stood in the doorway.

"Morning, Sister," she yawned. "Goin' to be a nice one – bit of sun to come, I shouldn't wonder – " From behind the screens round Mrs. Innes' bed, the older nurse from the children's ward appeared, carrying the chart that usually hung at the foot of the bed.

She padded over to Barbara, and looked anxiously into the shadowed white face.

"Mrs. Innes – she died about half an hour ago, Sister. I've sent for Doctor Foreman to see her and write the certificate and all – "

Barbara stared at her, uncomprehendingly. "Mrs. Innes – died? Mrs. Innes – ?"

And then the tears came, hot and harsh, tearing her weary body till she shook. She hardly knew why she was crying. It was morning. There was a bit of sun to come. Mary was dead, and Mrs. Innes had died half an hour ago. And Barbara wept like a baby, leaning against the wall where the patients couldn't see her, mourning for something she hardly understood.

Chapter Eight

The sun poured across the drawing-room, lighting the deep purple of the couch into a rich pool of colour. There was a thin layer of dust on the low bleached coffee-table, and the thick lilac rug beside it was rucked and crooked. Automatically Barbara leaned down and pulled it straight.

"You – you won't make strange, now, will you Barbara?" Geoffrey's tired voice sounded thin and uneven. "We – the children and I – we would like you to visit us as often as – as often as you care to – "

Barbara looked up at him, at the narrow shoulders in their stark black covering, at the vivid white of his shirt against neat black tie. She couldn't look at his face.

"No, of course not, Geoffrey. I'll visit you all as often as I can. How – how is Josie today?"

He shrugged. "Much the same. I can't get a word out of her. Doctor Maxwell has given me some sedative stuff for her at night, and it seems to have stopped the nightmares. But I wish she'd – show something – "

Barbara nodded. In the week since Mary's death, Josie had said little, speaking only when it was unavoidable. Each night she had woken screaming from nightmares, to cling desperately to Barbara who came running in to her from her own room across the

90

corridor. But in the morning again, she behaved as though Barbara and her father were strangers, pulling back sharply if Barbara happend to touch her in passing, sometimes staring at her father with lack-lustre eyes that held a glint of – was it dislike? in their pale depths.

Jamie's response to the news had been more orthodox. He had wept the agonised tears of the adolescent boy, stormy tears, but once this was over, he had seemed almost himself. He had retreated a little more perhaps into his private life, spending long hours at his friends' homes, but his attitude to his father remained unchanged – cool and friendly, accepting him as a man who had his own affairs to concern him, slipping easily into a comfortable male relationship that seemed to hold little of emotion in it.

"Jamie will be all right," Barbara had thought, watching him, smiling back as he caught her eye in a friendly little grin. "But Josie – Josie is taking this so badly – "

Barbara remembered, unwillingly, too much of what had gone before: Josie's bitter outburst against her mother, the way she had wished her mother dead – the possibility that she had seen and heard too much of what had happened the night of the party – the argument Barbara had had with Mary on the very last time they had spoken to each other – had Josie heard that? And she would push the memories away, confused and rather frightened, just as she had pushed away the thought of herself in Mary's place –

She stood up sharply, and still without looking at Geoffrey, spoke rapidly:

"I'll be going back to the hospital today, Geoffrey. Mrs. Lester will be moving into the attic flat with her husband this afternoon. She's used to the house, so it

91

shouldn't make – make too much difference. I mean – "
she floundered for a moment, and then recovered. "She
should be able to run the house quite smoothly for you.
If you need me at all, you'll let me know?"

"Yes – yes, thank you, my dear. It's been very good
of you to stay for this week. I've appreciated it. I don't
know what I'd have done without your help – so many
people at the funeral – " He grimaced suddenly, his face
creasing with pain. "Poor Mary – She'd have hated to
think – but I suppose it's a good way to – to go. Not knowing anything – " There was almost a question in his voice.

"She couldn't have known anything," Barbara said
gently. "Mr. Josephs said that too. Don't worry about
that, Geoffrey."

He walked across the room to stand staring out across
the sunlit garden. "I sometimes think this was my fault,"
he said abruptly. "If I hadn't been so wrapped up
in work, perhaps she wouldn't have spent so much
time with those damn committees. If I'd been better
company, she mightn't have gone to a meeting that
night – It might never have happened – "

"Don't be stupid!" Barbara's voice was sharp. "Mary
lived the life she wanted. She was happy. She wanted
you to work as you did – and she enjoyed her committee
work. Blaming yourself is ridiculous. And it won't help
Josie, either. She – well, I think perhaps she, too, is
feeling a sort of guilt – and she will need all the support
you can give her now."

He whirled round. "Josie, guilty? Why?"

Barbara evaded his eyes. "Children do get these ideas
– " She was purposely vague. "Especially girls of Josie's
age. If you can get her to talk – to cry – she'll be
better."

92

He sighed sharply. "I wish I could. I can't get near her, somehow. I'd hoped that perhaps you would be able to – "

"I'll try, Geoffrey. Give her more time for the – well, for her to realise what has happened. Then I'll try to see what I can do."

She went across to him, and held out her hand, looking at his face for the first time. "Goodbye, Geoffrey. I'll 'phone you in a day or so, to see how things are. And you can reach me if you need me."

He smiled at her, his thin face lighting for a moment. "Thank you again, Barbara. I'll try not to worry you unless I must. Take care of yourself, my dear. I – " he looked rueful. "I'd almost forgotten why you are here at all. How are you? Any more trouble with that ulcer?"

She smiled back. "Not too much – only if I miss a meal, or forget my pills." She had said nothing about the acute attack of pain that had followed the night that Mary had died, the almost perpetual feeling of vague ill health that had been with her all week. "I'm fine."

Together, they went to the front door. Barbara's small case stood there ready, and Geoffrey helped her into her coat.

As she buttoned it round her, Geoffrey put both hands on her shoulders, and smiled down into her face.

"I mean it, you know, Barbara. I *do* want you to come to see us often. We – I'll need you. You're a breath of fresh air and common sense, and that's – valuable." He leaned down and kissed her cheek gently, in a brotherly way. Barbara, almost to her surprise, didn't pull back, forgetting completely the strain that had existed between them since the party that had led to her leaving the house before. She just smiled up at him, and put out her hand to touch his cheek, sympathy bubbling up in her, uncomplicated sympathy.

Behind them, on the stairs, there was a faint rustle, and Barbara turned her head sharply to see Josie standing on the bottom step.

Her heart seemed to contract as she looked at the child. She had always been thin, always pale, but now she looked so fragile that a breath of wind could blow her away.

"Josie, darling," she said gently. "I must go back to the hospital today. But I'll be back to visit you all – and any time you'd like to see me, come along to the hospital – "

"Goodbye, Auntie Bar," Josie said dully. "Thank you for helping us." But there was no feeling behind the words. She said them automatically, just as any well-brought-up child would thank a hostess after a party. And with a little bob of her fair hair, she turned and went back up the stairs. Barbara watched her go, biting her lip.

"I know," said Geoffrey, unexpectedly. "I feel helpless too. Perhaps I'd better take her to see someone – a child psychologist – "

"Not yet. Give her time," Barbara said. "Time may help – "

But all the way back to the hospital, she worried about Josie. Of course she was distressed – any twelve-year-old, faced with such a dreadful shock, would be. But Josie's response to the shock was so odd, so unchildlike. "She's more like an old woman than a child," Barbara thought wretchedly. "And yet so vulnerable – "

The hospital felt like home when she came through the wide door into the main hall, and dropped her little suitcase beside the table in the centre of the stone-flagged floor. The smell of the place, the mixture of coffee and roast meat, of disinfectant and floor polish, was almost like a benison. Matron, hearing her footsteps on the stone, came bustling out of her cluttered office, to greet her like a long lost relative.

"Sister Hughes! Oh, my dear, but I'm glad to see you. Are you well? And how are they all? Poor Mr. Martin – such a loss – and the children, bless their little souls, how are they taking it? Come and have some sherry with me, you look worn out, child – come along now – "

And she swept Barbara away, to feed her sherry, and then some soup and an omelette, cooked by Matron herself, before taking Barbara up to her room to "see her settled comfortably again" as she put it in her breathless motherly fashion. And Barbara, only a little irritated by her questions, almost amused by the way she never waited for an answer to those questions, relaxed and allowed herself to be mothered.

Work again, she told herself, when she had finally managed to get rid of Matron, and was making a fresh cap and preparing her uniform, work was the answer. With plenty to do, she would have no time to remember the dreadful night that Mary had died, nor time to think about her own problems, of Josie and Geoffrey and Jamie. The summer season was about to start, and as Matron had once said, "In the summer, we do as much work here as any big Infirmary – wretched holiday crowds – we're run off our feet."

Barbara was looking forward to being "run off her feet".

Chapter Nine

"Dear Matron,

How nice it was to hear from you! I must confess that I felt very guilty when I got your letter; I should have written to you sooner. My only excuse is the pressure of work here. We may have only thirty beds, but the turnover has been tremendous – we've practically had patients queuing up for admission! It isn't always like this, I gather – just in the summer, when the town fills with holiday crowds. So, what with wards bulging with patients, and a steady influx into our tiny Casualty Department, I haven't had time to call my soul my own!

"Thank you for your very kind enquiries about my family. My young nephew seems to be quite well and happy, working hard for his University entrance. Josie, my niece, is, I am afraid, more of a problem. Even three months after her mother's death, she seemed to be still in a state of shock. The family doctor advised my brother-in-law to send her to a very good boarding-school he knew, where they have experience in helping these disturbed children. So, she went there. According to her headmistress, she has settled down there quite well – in fact, the head suggested that Josie should spend the first holiday away from home, going to

Switzerland with some of the other schoolgirls. So, when she comes home for Christmas holidays next month, it will be the first time we have seen her for five months! I do hope we shall find her more happy – her letters have been so short and uncommunicative, we haven't been able to assess for ourselves how she is.

"By all means give my regards to Doctor Marston. I suppose it *was* rather childish of me to have parted from an old friend on such bad terms. I do realise now that he acted in good faith, but I was too angry at the time to think clearly. I could have written, I suppose, but I really have been so very busy –

"I am feeling extremely well now, thank you. I have had no trouble with this dreary ulcer for some five months now – in fact, I rather think the thing has healed for good and all. I have been feeling so well, in fact, that I have been thinking that I should be able to return to the Royal – if you'll have me, that is – quite soon. The trouble is, I just wouldn't have the heart to leave Matron Elliott yet. She has the usual difficulty in finding and keeping nursing staff, and to leave now, even though the summer rush is coming to an end at last, would be rather selfish of me.

"I must say that this so-called "summer rush" is a remarkably long one. It started in April and here we are at the end of October, still dealing with holiday makers! What will never cease to surprise me is the number of women who decide to take a holiday during the last fortnight of pregnancy. We have had nineteen deliveries – emergency ones – this summer!

"Thank you again for your letter. It was like actually being at the Royal to read it. I feel positively homesick for the noise and bustle of North London. My best wishes to you all – "

Barbara signed the last sheet neatly, and stretched her tired back with a sigh. It had been a long day, and now, the evening mist was rising from the sea, and filling her room with the melancholy smell of autumn. She went over to her window, and leaned out for a brief moment, sniffing the mixed smells of fallen rotting leaves and chrysanthemums from the garden, and the ever present sea beyond. Then, she closed it, drew the curtains, and went down the corridor to run her bath.

As she relaxed in the hot water, she thought back again over the past seven months. It didn't seem so long, in some ways, but in others, it seemed as though she had spent her whole life at Sandleas Cottage Hospital. Every stick and stone of the old building was as familiar as the lines of her own hands; every patient and staff member were like old friends. In fact, she had hardly thought about the Royal for months, not until Matron Spencer had written to her so unexpectedly, the first letter since the correct letter of condolence she had written to Barbara after Mary's death.

It had been an odd seven months, Barbara thought, as she soaped herself. She had done little more than work, spending what off duty was left at the end of the day in reading, or the very occasional visit to the local repertory company. Apart from the regular Friday evening visit to the Martin house, that had been the sum total of her private and social life.

Fridays, Barbara mused. Odd evenings in many

ways. Mrs. Lester would serve dinner to Geoffrey, Jamie and herself, while they made desultory small talk, about Jamie's school activities (though he wasn't very forthcoming about them), about the hospital, about local happenings. Then they would drift into the drawing room, and watch television, while Jamie sat immersed in a book, and Geoffrey tried to relax while doing nothing. Poor Geoffrey. For so many years work had filled his life so completely that relaxation had become an effort. Barbara smiled a little wryly. It was clear now that Mary had been the driving force behind Geoffrey. Since her death, he had delegated more and more work to his staff, so that although he still held his position as the town's foremost solicitor, although as far as Barbara could tell his income remained at its old high level, he no longer tried to increase his practice, no longer sought after new clients. He had become a man who spent his evenings in his own home, instead of in his office or buried in paper-work brought from the office.

Clearly, the change suited him. He wasn't as uneasy in his inactivity as he had been at first, and his face had smoothed out, somehow, the lines of strain disappearing. He had even gained weight.

Barbara, with an effort, pulled herself out of her reverie, and began to dress. Friday today, and if she didn't hurry, she would be late for dinner, and that would make Mrs. Lester sulk.

The house felt warm and comfortable as she let herself in with the key Geoffrey had insisted on giving her. The hall was redolent of the rich smell of roast duckling, and she could see a log fire throwing leaping shadows over the drawing room walls. It was late – nearly half-past seven, so she went straight into the dining-room.

99

Geoffrey was sitting in his usual place at the head of the table, his face abstracted as he played with the soup spoon beside him. He looked up as Barbara came in, his face breaking into pleasure at the sight of her.

"Hello, my dear! Not too hard a day, I hope?"

"Thank you, no." Barbara slipped into her seat and unfolded her napkin, raising her eyebrows a little as she noticed that the table was only set for two.

"No Jamie tonight?"

"He's gone to the theatre with a friend of his, so I staked them to dinner at the Queen's. He's growing up fast, that boy, but he's still young enough to prefer an indifferent meal at a glossy hotel to a better one at home," he grinned lopsidedly. "I find it hard to realise I'm the father of quite so – so *large* a young man!"

Barbara laughed. Jamie was indeed a large young man, nearly six foot tall, and still growing, his raw frame beginning to fill out with muscle instead of childish gawkiness.

"Between ourselves," Geoffrey said, leaning back a little so that Mrs. Lester could serve his soup, "I suspect that this friend he is escorting is a female one. He was a little too forthcoming about the evening, somehow! When Jamie starts to tell me details about a 'chap at school' I can't help but be suspicious. It's so out of character!"

"It's time he did start showing an interest in girls," Barbara said serenely. "I would worry far more about a boy of seventeen who didn't."

"Wise Barbara!" Geoffrey laughed. "So un-Aunt-like a comment. You're quite right, of course. It is time he started looking at girls. That's why I staked him. I'm all for it!"

They ate their dinner in companionable silence. The duck was succulent, the vegetables properly cooked, the lemon mousse chilled to perfection. Barbara smiled at Mrs. Lester as she collected the last of the pudding plates.

"You cook like an angel, Mrs. Lester," she said, despising herself a little for her somewhat sycophantic smile. But keeping Mrs. Lester happy paid big dividends in comfort for Jamie and Geoffrey, she knew. "I wish I could."

Mrs. Lester bridled a little and preened herself. "Glad to teach you, Miss Hughes, any time. Just you come along to the kitchen, and I'll be there."

"I may well do that one of these days – when I have the time. Coffee in here or in the drawing-room, Geoffrey?"

"Oh, in the drawing-room, I think. Then we won't hold Mrs. Lester up in here."

Barbara, still thinking of keeping Mrs. Lester happy, collected the coffee tray from the kitchen herself, and carried it into the drawing-room. As she set it down on the low table and settled herself onto her favourite low pouffe on the hearth-rug she said casually, "What has television to offer tonight? The usual pattern, or something new?"

"Actually, I wanted to talk to you about something, Barbara." Geoffrey's voice sounded stilted, and Barbara looked up at him sharply. "Would you mind if we didn't watch tonight?"

"Not in the least! I thought you enjoyed it." Barbara said a little wonderingly.

"Sometimes – thank you." He took his coffee from her, and sat stirring it, his eyes gazing unseeingly into space, then he roused himself, and reached into his pocket.

"I've had a letter from Westchester," he held out a typewritten sheet. "The headmistress wanted me to come and see her before Josie started her holiday, but I couldn't get there – so she's written instead. I'd like you to read this."

Barbara took the letter, and smoothed it over her knees, straining her eyes to read it in the firelight. After a few preliminary comments about speech day, and the arrangements made for Josie to come home for the holiday, Miss Le Courbet had written " – I hope you will forgive what might seem impertinent advice; I would not offer it if I did not have Josephine's best interests at heart. I have been sorely worried about this child. She was so withdrawn, so *elderly* in her attitudes when she came to us, and I quite understood what a dreadful experience she had suffered, and the trauma caused by her mother's tragic and sudden death. Now that I have had the opportunity to observe Josephine for some months and, I hope, to build some sort of a relationship with her, I flatter myself I have been able to make some assessment of her needs.

"I fully realise, of course, the problems of a widower in caring for his children, and equally understand how your own sense of loss might make the arrangement of your household a difficult task for you. Josephine has told me of Mrs. Lester, and I am sure she is a very estimable housekeeper. But – forgive me – are you sure that she is an adequate person to give Josephine the feminine – indeed motherly – care that she so sorely needs? She is at such a difficult age. She really needs someone who can care for her as her mother would

102

have done had she been spared. If it were possible for you to find some kindly intelligent woman to take over this task, I feel that Josephine could overcome this sad period in her life, and grow into the adjusted and happy adult she has the potential to become. Again, do forgive me if I have been impertinent. I simply feel that there are occasions, as with this, when an interested outsider can see a problem more clearly."

Barbara slowly folded the letter, and gave it back to Geoffrey. There was a long silence, broken only by the crackle of the burning logs, and the distant clatter of dishes being washed in the kitchen.

Barbara broke the silence. "Well?" she said levelly. He bit his lip, and then stood up.

"A drink, I think – " he poured a glass of brandy for himself, and brought Barbara a little glass of the Drambuie he knew she liked.

She put it down on the table beside her, and sat, hands folded on the deep green of her dress, her dark head tilted a little as she looked up at him where he stood staring down into the fire, the leaping flames highlighting the bones of his cheeks, throwing his eyes into deep shadow so that she could not see the expression in them.

"I have – a suggestion to make, Barbara. Please, will you let me make it, and hear me out before you say anything?"

She nodded, never taking her eyes from his face.

"Miss Le Courbet's letter has merely made me an opportunity to speak to you on this – I have been thinking about it for some time, but I haven't known how or when to speak to you. I – I feel that Josie's needs are of prime importance, of course. But so, perhaps to a

103

lesser degree, are mine and Jamie's. He is nearly off my hands, I know. He will be at University next year, and living his own life. But Josie and I – we – " he fumbled for words, "we – dammit, to be honest, mostly I – am lonely. I admit that Mary and I weren't as – close as we might have been, but we complemented each other in many ways. I miss her presence – her companionship, if you like, more than I thought I would. I am not a man who can be sufficient to himself. I need someone to whom I can turn for advice, who can support me both in my business life and my private life. You must have noticed that I work less well than I once did. The practice has not suffered because of this – yet. But it will, I think, if I don't do something more active soon." He turned and looked down at her, "Barbara – to be straightforward, my dear, I am asking you to marry me."

Chapter Ten

She didn't move. They stayed there in the same positions, frozen into immobility, Geoffrey looking down at her anxiously, where she sat still and quiet at his feet. Then she stirred and raised her head.

He smiled his lopsided smile. "Please, don't misunderstand me. This is no – romantic whim. I could, I think, have asked you to come to live in this house, to care for my home and children, merely as the children's aunt, and I suspect you would have come on those terms. You have a strong sense of duty, haven't you? You would have felt a moral – obligation – to come. But that would be unfair. I couldn't ask you to give up your own life for me and my children's welfare. As my wife, I can offer you – material well-being, security – status, if you like, something you would not have as a – well – as a glorified housekeeper. I would not insult you with such a proposal."

Barbara nodded gravely. "I see. Then this – proposal of marriage is a – "

"A friendly businesslike arrangement if you like." He broke away from her, turning to throw another log on the fire. It burst into a shower of sparks, lighting his face vividly for a moment. "You would of course, have your – your own room. I do not expect – more –

than companionship – " He looked at her appealingly. "Do you understand what I'm trying to say, Barbara? I'm not finding this easy."

She was quiet for a moment, then she said levelly.

"I think I do. You propose a companionate marriage. Romantic love has no part of it. To be blunt, we live together, but we do not sleep together." Barbara was a little surprised at her own even voice, at the coolness she both felt and displayed.

He flushed. "Perhaps I am equally unfair to suggest that. I don't know. But – you are so – so serene, so sufficient to yourself. I – have no way of knowing whether you feel you need – more than this from a marriage. Children of your own, perhaps – "

His voice died away, then strengthened again. "I just thought that you could well have made a romantic marriage years ago had you wanted to. You are beautiful." She shook her head impatiently. "You are, even if you don't realise it. But that isn't important – what I mean is that I've thought about this very carefully. And it seemed to me that you might – understand this suggestion."

She put her arms round her knees and stared into the fire. "When I lived in this house for a few days last April, one of the biggest problems I had to face was that I envied Mary." She looked up at him a little ruefully. "I am trying to be honest with you, you see. I envied her her home, her children – particularly Josie, for whom I have a – a – great deal of affection. I enjoyed the comfort of this house, the sense of security it carried. And I despised myself for it. And now – " she shook her head in confusion. "What you suggest now offers me just what I wanted then. This

106

makes it difficult for me to – consider accepting. Can you understand that?"

He nodded gravely. "I think I can. But you need have no – guilt about feeling like this. It is very natural – very practical, if you like."

"Guilt," she frowned briefly. "There is that, too. I feel I owe you and Josie something. I can't explain why. I just do. It is this that makes me inclined to accept."

He leaned forward eagerly. "Whatever your reasons for accepting, Barbara, I hope you will. You need not feel that you owe us anything at all – I can't imagine how you possibly could – but I would be happier if you accepted on those terms than if you refused me on any others."

"I must think – " The room slid into silence again. She sat still, trying to collect her thoughts in some sort of order. It was true that Geoffrey was offering her something she had once wanted. Security, status, Josie. She looked round the room, at the cool bleached wood, the rich purple of the upholstery, and wondered. Did she still want this? And above all, did she want Josie?

It was harder to decide the answer to this. When Josie had said, so long ago it seemed now, that she wanted Barbara to be her mother, there had been no doubt. Barbara, too, wanted Josie. But now? Josie was different – how different there would be no way of knowing until she came home for the holidays. But then Barbara remembered Miss Le Courbet's letter. *She* thought Josie needed a mother to replace Mary. Would the child accept Barbara?

And what of herself? Suppose she refused this proposal? Barbara tried to visualise her life in the future as Sister Hughes. Years of hard work, to end in what? A Matronship perhaps. And afterwards? A lonely retirement, no longer needed by anyone when her working days were over. She remembered nursing a retired nurse once, a lonely old lady, who seemed to have no reason for living once her working days had ended. Was this what she wanted?

She shivered for a moment. She had never thought much about the future before. Now she was being forced to. Perhaps, if she refused Geoffrey, she would one day marry someone else – a "romantic" marriage as Geoffrey had called it.

"But is that likely?" part of her mind sneered. "Geoffrey says you are beautiful – but you are thirty, and you have never yet been asked to marry anyone, have you?"

She argued with herself, "I've had men friends – "

"Oh, yes," sneered the silent voice in her mind. "Daniel Marston was one, wasn't he? There was a time you thought – "

But this was a dangerous thought. Daniel had gone out of her life seven months before. He had made no attempt to contact her – whatever she may once have thought about him had died. So she raised her head and looked at Geoffrey, standing silently in front of the fire.

"Thank you for your suggestion, Geoffrey," she said levelly. "I think, with you, that this arrangement has much to commend it. I – I will marry you."

He straightened as though a heavy load had suddenly slipped from his back.

"Thank you, my dear," he said softly.

Then he switched on the bright centre light, throwing the room in vivid relief. The pool of firelight in which they had been sitting dwindled away.

108

"We must discuss arrangements." He was brisk. "I shall arrange for a marriage settlement to be drawn up – "

"A settlement?"

"Of course! I feel strongly that this is necessary. Both the children have money settled on them, to which they will have access when they come of age. I propose to settle some ten thousand pounds on you, the interest to be yours from the time we marry, the capital to be completely yours on my death. I will, of course, also change my will when we marry."

"I see," she murmured. This sudden transition to talk of money confused her. She was embarrassed, too, and Geoffrey seemed to sense this.

"Better to settle all this now," he said gently. "Then we need not think of it again. Part of this arrangement is to offer you security, isn't it? This is how I intend to – to implement that part of the arrangement."

"Very well." She schooled her voice so that it was as business-like as his own. "But whatever arrangements you make, I would not like the children to suffer any – any – financial loss on my account."

"They won't, I assure you. Their financial future was planned years ago. They are well cared for. And Mary had some money of her own, too, you remember. The children have that completely."

Barbara *had* forgotten. Their parents had left little to Barbara, perhaps because she was not married. They had left a considerable sum to Mary in trust for her children.

Geoffrey was talking again. "You will have two bank accounts when we marry. One will be for the household expenses, all of which I will ask you to deal with for me.

The other will be your own allowance. I would suggest five hundred a year?"

She blinked, "If you wish." This was horribly embarrassing, but Geoffrey went on:

"I carry considerable life insurance, so I think I can safely say you will be comfortably off should I leave you a widow. And this house will be yours, too."

"Whatever you say, Geoffrey. I would rather not know, quite honestly – "

"But you must! It is all part of the arrangement." He smiled at her. "But I think that is all I have to tell you. I shall have to ask you for your signature on various documents, of course, but not until later." For a moment, his briskness left him. "Er – have you any preferences about – when we should marry?"

"Oh – " this brought it all so very close that she almost panicked, almost said she had changed her mind. "Oh – I hadn't thought – "

"I wondered if perhaps in May? That gives us six months for the children to become accustomed to the idea – and will stop any tendency to local gossip. People seem to place some magical meaning on the passing of a year. If we married before – before the anniversary of Mary's death, there would be unpleasant talk. If we wait until May, there will be less. There is sure to be some, of course – "

Barbara nodded. "I suppose there will," she said evenly. "But if you are not bothered by it, I certainly shan't be. It's the children I worry about."

"Yes – " He ran a hand over his face. "I don't think Jamie will be any problem – but Josie – "

"We can only wait until we see her next month," Barbara said decisively. "I think you might tell Jamie, but we will suggest that he says nothing to Josie till we do. I think he'll understand."

"Yes – " He smiled suddenly. "You see? Already you are helping me with decisions! Thank you again, Barbara. I hardly hoped you would accept – but I can't tell you how pleased I am that you have. As long as you are sure that this – will be enough of a marriage for you – "

"I have accepted, Geoffrey," she said quietly. "Leave it at that."

"Very well. I don't want to invade your private thoughts completely – you must still feel free – "

She felt weary suddenly, filled with a need for solitude.

"If you will forgive me, Geoffrey, I think perhaps I'll go back to the hospital now. I know it's early, but – " she said a little awkwardly.

"Of course, my dear. I quite understand. I'll drive you – "

They said little on the drive to the hospital. When Geoffrey stopped the car outside the main entrance and hurried round the car to open her door, she knew a moment of panic. Would he try to kiss her, perhaps? But then she remembered. This was not that sort of engagement.

"I'm engaged!" she thought in a kind of dumb surprise, as she got out of the car. "Engaged to be married!" and the thought was so suddenly, so exquisitely funny, that she laughed aloud.

He looked puzzled, even worried, by her laughter. "So sorry," she said lamely. "I – I caught my foot in the door and nearly fell. That's why I laughed – "

His face cleared, and he took one of her hands in both

of his own. "Goodnight, Barbara," he said softly. "And thank you." And with a brief tightening of his grasp, he let her go, and went back to the car, to drive smoothly away into the October darkness.

Barbara, suddenly exhausted, drained of any feeling, climbed the stairs to her room. Matron's sitting room door was open, light spilling across the polished floor of the corridor.

On an impulse she went towards it. She needed a woman to talk to, needed someone to talk to desperately. And Matron Elliott, with her bustling ways, her comfortable talk and her shrewd commonsense was just the person she needed.

She pushed the sitting room door open, and stood blinking in the light for a moment.

"Sister!" Matron pulled herself out of the chair beside the little hearth, grunting a little with the effort. "Just the girl I wanted to see! Back early – wonderful! My dear, I have a surprise for you! An old friend of yours is here – "

She waddled over to the door, to pull on Barbara's cold hands, urging her into the room. The other chair by the fireside, the one that had its back to the door, moved a little as its occupant, hidden from Barbara's sight, moved slightly.

Matron Elliott led Barbara to the fireside, turning her triumphantly on the hearth-rug to face the other easy chair.

"There!" she said joyfully. "What do you think of *that*?"

Sitting in the chair, his dark red head settled deeply into his shoulders, his lazy eyes crinkling up at her, sat Daniel Marston.

112

Chapter Eleven

"Hello, Barbara," he smiled at her, and got to his feet, to come and stand beside her, taking her own cold hands in his. "Have you forgiven me?"

"How characteristic," Barbara thought in an oddly detached way. "We don't meet for seven months – we don't even write to each other, and now he carries on just as though we had met yesterday." Aloud, she said, "Daniel! What are you doing here?"

"One question at a time!" his smiled broadened. "My answer first. Have you forgiven me?"

"Oh, of course! I was furious with you at the time, I know, but I'd have to be pretty adolescent to carry on being angry after all this time, wouldn't I?" She peered up at him a little impishly. "Particularly as you were right – I *was* ill, I suppose – and I'm fine now. So I'll have to admit I was wrong as gracefully as I can!"

He made a mock fist, and pretended to swipe at her jaw, a familiar gesture that brought all the past flooding back, and made her feel as though she, too, had seen him only yesterday.

"That's my girl! And I, for my part, apologise for being so dam' hamfisted about the whole business. I've as much tact as a bulldozer. Sorry, Bar!"

Matron Elliott, almost purring in her pleasure,

beamed happily at them. "Well, now, you two must want to talk your heads off. I'm away to a bath and bed – you stay here, now, and help yourselves – whisky here, Doctor Marston, and sherry, and I think there are a few biscuits – " She bustled about her little room, finding glasses and bottles and a tin of biscuits, settling them both in the easy chairs each side of the fire, throwing more coal on to the already blazing grate, and generally behaving like a mother hen.

When she had gone, closing the door behind her with elephantine tact, they sat and stared at each other. Barbara felt a sudden constraint as she looked at the face opposite, so familiar, and yet so strange.

He bent forward to the little table Matron had pulled to his side, and started to fix himself a drink with the absorbed expression on his face that he always brought to even the smallest of tasks.

Barbara leaned back in her chair and watched him, trying to assess her feelings as she did so. She felt oddly mixed. Part of her was filled with unadulterated pleasure at meeting an old friend again, and at finally clearing up a foolish argument. But another part of her felt panic, sheer stupid panic. In her usual cool clear-headed fashion, Barbara tried to analyse this feeling. Why should she feel so afraid to see him? What was it that made her want to run and hide from him?

He leaned back in his chair, cradling his drink in his hands, after he had put a glass of Matron's dubious sherry in front of her.

"Your question now. I'm here to study, mainly. I'm trying my Mastership in Surgery in a few months – and I've got enough solid experience under my belt to concentrate on book work for a while. I looked for

114

a peaceful job somewhere where I could get enough time for that. So I applied for this post. The boy you've had here is going on to Dover, I gather – I start duty tomorrow." He looked up at her and laughed suddenly.

"D'you know something? I hadn't the remotest idea that this was *your* Cottage Hospital till that old duck of a Matron happened to mention your name – in the middle of a lot of other chatter – "

Barbara laughed too. "Mmm. She does run on, doesn't she? But don't let her fool you. She's a top-rate nurse, and she's the perfect Matron for a place like this. Got the hospital at her finger ends – it's a happy place – "

He nodded. "You can feel that the minute you put your foot through the door. I'm looking forward to the next six months. And the duck assures me the heavy work is over for the year, so I'll have plenty of time to do my own work as well as the hospital's. Now – " He leaned forward and smiled crookedly at her. "Enough about me. What's with you? Tell me everything that's happened to you. How's the ulcer?"

A little shy suddenly, Barbara lit a cigarette, making much of the small action. "Me? I'm fine – the ulcer seems to have gone completely now. I'll have a barium meal in a month or so, to make sure, but I don't expect there'll be anything wrong – "

"And your family? You have a sister here, haven't you? I seem to remember Matron at the Royal saying something about – "

"She's dead," Barbara said baldly. "She was – killed in a road accident just after I came here."

There was a moment's shocked silence. Then Daniel

said awkwardly, "I'm sorry, Barbara. I had no idea. Forgive a clumsy question."

She shrugged. "It's all right. I can't pretend to be dreadfully upset – not for Mary, that is. I – we weren't very close, I'm afraid. It was worse for the children, really – "

He nodded soberly. "How are they? Are they very young?"

She told him about Josie and Jamie, talking a great deal about them. Anything not to talk about Geoffrey.

And it was as she realised that she didn't want to talk about Geoffrey that she also realised why she had felt panic at the sight of Daniel. How could she explain to him about her engagement to Geoffrey? Daniel, with his clean integrity, who had never had any use for anything but the same integrity in others – how could he understand what she was doing?

"To an outsider," she thought drearily, staring into the fire, after her own voice had come to a stop. "To an outsider it'll look like simple opportunism. I've accepted a proposal of marriage from a man fifteen years older than I am – a man I don't love – I've contracted myself to a marriage of convenience for us both. He provides for his and his children's comfort. I provide for my own security and – financial future." She felt sick at the thought.

"But it isn't like that at all," she argued with herself. "It's Josie, really. That's why I'm marrying Geoffrey."

But however much Josie's needs came into it, there was no escaping the facts. She had wanted security, Mary's home and position, and now she was going to get just that.

Daniel stood up suddenly. "You're tired, love," he

116

said gently. "We'll talk some more tomorrow – six months of tomorrows. Bed for you now. Come on."

He pulled her to her feet, and with an arm across her shoulders led her to the door. "I'll see you on duty tomorrow morning. And maybe we'll have time to go out in the afternoon, mmm? You can show me this town and we'll see what we can plan in the way of entertainment for ourselves this weekend. Matron says we're both off duty. Away with you now – " and he pushed her gently away before clattering off cheerfully to his own room down the corridor, turning at his door to wave briefly to her.

She slept fitfully that night. Too much had happened too suddenly for clear thought. Engaged to Geoffrey – Josie to face with the news, and now Daniel, like a sudden gust of wind on a hot day, blowing her off her balance, so that she lost the equilibrium that seemed so much a part of her makeup.

When she came on duty the next morning, she felt a little better. The mere act of putting on her starched uniform was like putting on a sort of mental armour. While she was on duty she wouldn't have to think about herself and her own confused problems.

She escorted Daniel round the hospital, trying not to notice the way interest in his masculine good looks made even the older nurses smooth their uniform dresses over their hips, a little amused at the way the patients in the women's ward sat up straighter in their beds and slyly tweaked their hair into order as he came through the door.

He was clearly enchanted with the hospital, just as she had been herself when she had first come to it. He seemed to relax, to lose some of the stiffness that was so much a part of a Royal doctor, to become more of a person and less of a medical mind in a white coat.

There were a few patients for him in Casualty, a couple of out-patients to be seen, and one or two routine ward jobs. By lunchtime he had finished his day's work, and Matron Elliott, cheerfully doling out meat pies at the communal lunch table said, "Now, Sister Hughes. I'm on this afternoon, so you take Doctor Marston out and show him Sandleas. Not much to see, Doctor, I grant you, but a bit of sea air'll do you good after all that London rush you're used to. We'll make you as healthy to look at as we did Sister Hughes, I promise you! She was a peaky thing when she came here, and look at her now!"

The other nurses tittered dutifully, and stole sly looks at Barbara's flaming cheeks. Daniel laughed lazily, and grinned at Barbara.

"You've made a new woman of her, Matron!" he said wickedly. "I wouldn't have recognised her."

"And we'll do the same for you," Matron said comfortably. "You've plenty of time for all that studying you want to do, so you get out into the air this afternoon."

Barbara felt a little angry. However well Matron meant, her over-emphasis on their old friendship, the way she seemed determined to throw them together, embarrassed her. She *didn't* want to go out with Daniel that afternoon, didn't want to be alone with him. And with her usual honesty, Barbara knew why. Sooner or later she would have to tell him about Geoffrey, and she wanted to make it as late as possible.

But the problem was solved for her. As they left the dining room after lunch, to make way for the second sitting, the junior nurse from Casualty came panting up the corridor towards them. Matron had already waddled off to her office, so the nurse stopped in front of Barbara, and said breathlessly, "Please, Sister, there's a man in Casualty, looks very ill. Could you please come?"

With Daniel close behind her, she followed the nurse back to the little department. An ambulance man came out of the small cubicle at the back of the room, and nodded impartially at them both.

"Afternoon, Doctor – Sister. Picked this bloke up on the Front. Thought he was drunk at first, but I'm not so sure now – "

They pushed the curtain aside, and went in to stand beside the couch to look down on the white unshaven face of an elderly man. He was rolling his head from side to side and groaning, his knees drawn up, his face twisted with pain. Gently, Daniel straightened the bent legs, and with quick fingers unbuttoned his clothes to expose the abdomen. The man opened his eyes, and attempted a smile before creasing his face back into the lines of pain.

"Awful belly ache – " he muttered.

Daniel's examination was quick and thorough. He asked a few concise questions, nodding at the old man's confused answers. As his stethoscope moved over the bony chest and then over the distended abdomen, Barbara, preparing notes and a chart for Daniel, noticed, almost unwillingly, the way his square shoulders moved under the white coat, the crisply curling hair at the nape of his neck, the sharp lines of his profile. How could she have forgotten how attractive he was?

Daniel straightened and, with a friendly pat on the old man's shoulder, held the curtain aside for Barbara to precede him out into the Casualty room.

119

"He's got an obstruction – pretty low one, I think. He'll need surgery. Can you manage a laparotomy here, or must he be moved to Dover?"

"We can manage," Barbara said. "I'll set up – Nurse!"

As Daniel went back to explain to the patient what was to be done, Barbara sent the little nurse scuttling off to arrange for a bed to be prepared in the ward and to tell Matron, before making her own way to the theatre.

As she laid up, methodically preparing the instruments and trolleys, she felt almost guilty at her sense of relief. It was tough on the old man of course, but Barbara was truly grateful for his obstruction. Now she would be able to shelve the difficult afternoon tête-à-tête with Daniel.

Matron put her head round the door, holding one end of her veil over her mouth as a sort of mask.

"Shall I take this, Sister?" she asked in a muffled voice. "It's your half day – "

"I don't mind," Barbara said cheerfully. "If you took it, I'd still have to stay on to cover the rest of the hospital. And you know I like theatre – "

"Bless you, m'dear." Matron was relieved. "It isn't one of my fortes, I must say. Doctor Marston'll be better served if you're here. I'll send a junior to run," and she scuttled off, her shoes clacking busily along the corridor outside.

The operation went smoothly. The local G.P. who came to do anaesthetics arrived in plenty of time, and an hour after the old man had first arrived at the hospital, he was on the table being sheeted up by Barbara, while Daniel scrubbed his strong brown forearms at the sink in the corner.

Daniel was an even better surgeon than she had

remembered, Barbara thought, watching the strong square fingers working. As she slapped instruments into his outstretched hand and threaded needles for him, Barbara felt happier than she had for a long time. This was the work she was meant for – all that she ever really wanted to do. And she pushed the implications of the thought aside to concentrate on the work in hand.

Daniel found the obstruction, and grunted a little as he saw the extent of the damage it had done.

"I'll have to do a resection, Sister," he said. "Have you the gear, or do you need time to get it ready?"

"It's all here," Barbara said, unable to avoid letting a little note of pride from creeping into her voice.

Daniel winked at the anaesthetist. "Such a theatre sister!" he murmured. And the anaesthetist smiled back, and nodded happily at Barbara. "We're lucky to have her here, Doctor," he said. "We're all hoping she'll stay a good while too – "

The operation went on, Daniel resecting out the damaged portion of gut, making his anastomosis neatly, settling the drains carefully in place.

When the last stitch was in, and Barbara had put the dressing on, they stood back to watch him on his way out of the theatre, Matron bustling at the head of the trolley, the anaesthetist on the other side, watching the tired old face above the red blanket of the trolley.

"He'll do," Daniel said, satisfaction in his voice. "But I'm glad that ambulance man found him. Another couple of hours, and he mightn't have done so well. I'd give my eye teeth for a cuppa, Bar."

She stretched and laughed. "Me too. Look, Nurse, can you clear up here? I'll chase up some tea for Doctor Marston, and come back to check the instruments later."

It was like old times, she thought, sitting in an armchair in Matron's little office, a steaming cup of tea cradled in her hands. To sit in companionable silence after a difficult case, knowing that she had been as good as his right hand – just as it always had been. She sighed a small sigh of pleasure.

Daniel smiled across at her from his perch on Matron's cluttered desk.

"You enjoyed that, didn't you?" he said abruptly.

"Mmm. It's always good to get a tricky one, and know he's going to do," she said dreamily. "Makes it all so – worthwhile somehow."

"Barbara – " His voice sounded so odd, that she pulled her head up sharply to stare at him.

He was looking at her with an odd expression on his face, his eyes glinting a little under the line of hair that showed beneath the theatre cap pushed back over his head. Above the mask dangling under his chin, his mouth was very straight.

He dropped his eyes to stare down into his cup.

"If I get my Mastership, I'm going abroad," he said abruptly. "I've been offered a chance in a million. There's a hospital in Australia – out in the bush a bit – being built, and they want a chief of staff to get it going properly. They'll take me without the extra degree, but I want it because I think I'll do a better job if I get it."

He raised his head to stare at her, his eyes suddenly sombre. "I had it all worked out, you know. It was just what I wanted – a new hospital, plenty of chance to really develop a surgical set-up where it was desperately needed – I thought that was all I wanted. Until I came here."

122

She said nothing, staring up at him in a sort of hypnotic trance.

"I didn't know just how much I'd missed you until I saw you again yesterday, Bar. But I did. Dreadfully." He managed a smile. "You'd become a part of my life, and I'd hardly realised it."

"No – " she wanted him to stop, to go back to being his old ordinary self. She didn't like this – the way he was looking at her, the words that she knew were coming. "No – "

"Yes," he said gently. "You *are* a part of my life, Bar. I – " He looked like a little boy for a moment, and then jumped down from the desk, to come and stand above her chair, leaning down to look deeply into her eyes.

"Barbara – I love you. A great deal. Will you marry me and come out to the wilds with me?" His eyes laughed down into hers, pleading, but somehow confident.

She sat there in her chair, still clutching her cup in both hands, staring up at him, shakingly aware of his arms on each side of her as he rested his hands on the arms of her chair, feeling his warm breath on her face, smelling the achingly familiar mixture of ether and soap and tweed that was so much a part of him.

"Will you, Bar?" he said again, a fleeting line appearing between his eyes.

Behind him a door opened sharply. Daniel straightened, and turned his head angrily to stare at the intruder. From the depths of the chair Barbara could see beyond Daniel's stocky shape to the doorway framing Geoffrey. He stood there, his hat held tightly in one hand, the other diffidently, touching his tie.

"I'm so sorry," he said hesitantly. "The nurse outside said I would find Sister Hughes here – "

Barbara, pulled out of her trance, got to her feet.

"It'll all right, Geoffrey," she said. "Here I am. Anything wrong?"

His face lit up at the sight of her. "No – nothing wrong, my dear. But I thought you might be off duty this afternoon, so I came to see if you would care to come down to Westchester to see Josie – "

Daniel moved suddenly, and crossed the room to pick up his cup of tea again from the desk where he had left it. Geoffrey, a little puzzled, said again, "I'm so sorry – perhaps I'd better go – I didn't realise you weren't off duty – "

"I am now, I think – we just had an emergency operation, but it's finished. I've a bit of clearing up to do, but that isn't too much – " She was gabbling in her nervousness. Geoffrey, undecided, half turned to go, and Barbara put her hand out to pull him back. "Geoffrey – I'd like you to meet an old – friend of mine," she said, her voice sounding harsh in her own ears. "This is Daniel Marston, Geoffrey."

Daniel turned and came over to the door, his face smooth and expressionless again. "How do you do," he said, holding his hand out to Geoffrey.

"Geoffrey – " she felt her throat constrict suddenly, and swallowed. "Geoffrey and I are to be married, Daniel," she said, looking straight ahead of her. "We – it was decided yesterday evening."

Chapter Twelve

The silence was so thick it was almost palpable. Geoffrey looked at Barbara with a faint line between his brows, apparently unaware of the effect her statement had had on the man standing beside them. Then he said, "Er – I thought we weren't going to – "

"Oh, that's all right, Geoffrey." Barbara's voice was high and brittle. "You needn't worry about Daniel. He's a stranger to the town, so he's hardly likely to use this as gossip – and he's an old friend of mine."

Geoffrey's face cleared. "Then, of course – " and he turned to smile rather diffidently at Daniel.

"Forgive me," he said charmingly, "it's just that we – we hadn't intended to talk about this yet, for one reason and another, but of course, as an old friend – "

"My congratulations," Daniel's voice was harsh. "I hope you'll be very happy, both of you," and with a curt nod, he turned and left, the door swinging sharply closed behind him.

"Odd chap." Geoffrey stared at the door with irritation. "Is he always so brusque?"

"Oh – I don't know." Barbara turned to the mirror above the fireplace and pulled off her theatre cap, avoiding Geoffrey's eyes. "You wanted to go to see Josie today?"

"I thought it might be a good idea." He sat down and stretched his legs a little. "I was thinking, you see, and it did occur to me that however careful we were, someone might hear and tell her before we did – and that wouldn't be good, would it?"

"Who could tell her?"

"Well – Mrs. Lester, for one. I don't want to sound suspicious, but she's an inquisitive woman, and I've sometimes thought she was a bit more interested in my private affairs than she should be – I think she – " he made a face, "I think she listens at doors. And she's been behaving a bit oddly today already. So – "

"Yes – you're probably right." Barbara straightened. "Look, I'll have to see if Matron will finish clearing up for me – if she will, I'll be ready in about half an hour. Will that be all right?"

"Of course. I'll wait for you here, shall I?"

Later, as she sat beside Geoffrey in the car, driving the thirty miles to Josie's school, Barbara tried to think. Daniel, asking her to marry him –

"Oh, God," she thought drearily. "Why couldn't he have come sooner, before Geoffrey had asked me? Or why in hell couldn't he have stayed away?" For a moment, she almost hated Daniel, hated him for the way his proposal had made her heart leap dizzily, hated him for opening up a line of thought she had firmly killed years before.

There had been a time when she had wanted Daniel to love her, a time when she had dreamed about marriage to him, but as their friendship had continued along its old familiar lines, she had told herself that it was no more than friendship, and stifled her hopes. And now –

The car slid to a stop outside the tall old building in

its neat grounds, and Geoffrey turned off the engine and sat in silence for a second. Then he said, "It's ridiculous – I feel as nervous as a kitten. Almost as nervous as I did last night, when I spoke to you – she's a funny child – "

"Sitting here worrying won't help," Barbara said crisply. "We'd better see her, I suppose. Then we'll know where we are – "

He nodded, and got out of the car, to come round to open her door and help her out.

"Thank God for your calm good sense, Barbara. The more I see of it, the more grateful I am that you are – you're to be my wife."

Barbara didn't answer. She couldn't. "To be desirable for one's good sense," she thought wryly. "I wonder if that's what Daniel finds attractive – " and pushed the thought away.

Miss Le Courbet was charm itself. She was a smooth elegant woman, with an overpowering personality that made Barbara feel like a schoolgirl herself for a little while. She sat silently in the luxurious study while Geoffrey, with some embarrassment, explained why they had come, and what they wanted to tell Josie. Miss Le Courbet was clearly in delighted approval.

"I am so glad you took my suggestion so kindly, Mr. Martin," she said smoothly. "One sometimes fears that one's good intentions may be misconstrued. I am more than delighted for you both, of course, and that your decision should be one that will so obviously be to Josephine's benefit."

Barbara felt a little sick. The elegant woman was obviously in no misconception about the situation. Barbara and Geoffrey were to make a marriage of convenience, and she saw this as clearly as if she had been present in

127

Geoffrey's drawing-room the night before and had listened to his proposal. Barbara felt like a character in a Victorian novel, and hated herself for it.

But she had little time for thought; Miss Le Courbet sent for Josie, and with a sleek smile, left the three of them together in the big quiet study.

Josie stood at the door, her face paler than ever above the dark green of her uniform gym slip and white blouse.

"Hello, Daddy. Hello, Auntie Bar," she said. "How are you?"

"We're fine, dear." Geoffrey went across and kissed the cool cheek, and Josie made no more response than if he had been a fly alighting on her face. "And how are you?" His embarrassment made him stiff, even pompous. "Keeping well, I hope?"

"Yes thank you."

There was silence for a moment, Josie making no attempt to break it. "You've grown, darling," Barbara said, feeling foolish suddenly.

Josie nodded.

"You – you like it here?" Barbara tried again.

"Yes thank you."

"It seems very pleasant," Barbara said, trying to be bright. "Lovely grounds – "

"Yes."

Almost in desperation, Barbara said, "we – thought you might like to go out to tea. Is there somewhere near we could get a good tea, do you know?"

"Miss Le Courbet said there would be tea here for you later, and I have to have tea with the others," Josie said flatly. "Thank you."

Unexpectedly, Geoffrey took over.

"Jo – come and sit down. We want to talk to you, and it isn't easy with you standing there – " He smiled at her, almost appealingly. "Come and sit here with us."

Obediently, she came and perched herself on the edge of a chair to sit with hands folded on her lap staring solemnly at them both. Barbara, looking at her, felt a strange sense of fear. This wasn't the child she had expected to see. Somehow, subtly, Josie had changed. Even her face looked different. The thinness of months before had altered to a sort of asceticism, the bones of her face throwing blue shadows on to her cheeks, her eyes seeming more deepset and remote than they ever used to. Her pale spun-sugar hair was pulled back sleekly, showing the high white forehead. She looked for all the world like a painting of a medieval saint, and Barbara was surprised when the simile sprang into her mind.

Geoffrey was speaking:

"Josie – we came to tell you something important, my dear. We – your aunt and I – we – " He stumbled a little, "we are going to be married early next year, Josie, love. We want you to know and be happy about it."

She showed no sign of surprise, no flicker of interest. "I hope you will be very happy," she said after a small pause.

Barbara leaned forward anxiously. "Josie, darling, please – please, tell us what you feel about this. Do you mind? Do you dislike the idea, or – or are you glad for yourself?"

Josie looked directly at her, her blue eyes opaque.

"It doesn't make much difference to me, does it?" she said flatly. "It's up to you – nothing to do with me."

"Of course it's got something to do with you," Barbara

said almost violently. "It matters so much to you that I – we would be very distressed if you didn't like the idea. We – "

"Oh, you needn't worry," Josie said. "I'm not the sort to get into a state about things, not any more. I might have once – but – not any more."

Barbara could have cried at the elderly way she spoke, the way this child made her feel as though, to herself, life was an old, dull story. "No one of Josie's age should be so calm, so *sensible*," Barbara thought, almost weeping. "It's as though someone froze her – "

"Darling," Barbara said gently, "I'm not suggesting you get into a state. I'm just trying to find out how you feel about this – "

With sudden and unexpected tact, Geoffrey got up.

"I'll be back," he said briefly. "I want to see Miss Le Courbet – " and he went, leaving the two women, one so young yet so much a woman, alone together.

Josie made no sign, showing no interest in his going.

"Look, Josie," Barbara got up herself, and walked over to the window, staring out into the darkening afternoon light. "This marriage – " She could see Josie reflected against the glass of the window, and stared at the faint reflection as she went on. "I don't know really how much you know about marriage at all – why people get married, or what they want from a marriage." She ran a hand across her face briefly, and then went on, "For some, for – young people – marriage is an exciting and romantic thing. It will be for you, one day. But for others, it isn't like that – "

She turned to look directly at the silent figure on the edge of the chair.

"What I'm trying to tell you is that this – this marriage

130

– between your father and myself isn't a great romantic thing. I'm telling you this because I think it might help you to understand us better. I don't know how – " her voice was almost a cry, almost a plea for understanding. "Please, Josie, try to help me – we were – such friends once!"

"But it is a romantic thing," Josie said unexpectedly. "Why tell me lies? Why should you think it might make it better?"

Barbara almost ran across the room to fall on her knees in front of the child, to stare up into her face.

"It isn't!" she cried. "If it were, I wouldn't have said otherwise – you must see that! It's as much for you as for me and your father! I want to look after you all – you and Jamie – and if you'll let me take your mother's place as best I can – "

Josie stared down at her in the dimming light, expression – puzzled expression – on her face for the first time.

"For me?" she said wonderingly. "Me and Jamie?"

Barbara nodded eagerly. "Yes, darling – I love you both very much – and I want to see you happy and looked after. That's why – "

"I don't believe you," Josie said flatly.

"Why don't you? Have I ever lied to you before?"

"Not with words – "

"How else could I lie?" Barbara was appealing. "I don't know what you mean – "

Josie stood up suddenly, pushing past Barbara's kneeling figure to stand and stare down at her.

"It doesn't matter," she said dully. "I hope you'll both be happy," and silently she turned and walked out of the room, closing the door softly behind her.

131

"She saw us," Barbara thought, sick and miserable. "That damned party – she saw Geoffrey afterwards – "

The door opened softly again, and Geoffrey stood peering across the room before hurrying over to her side, to help her to her feet.

"Barbara! What happened? Where is she?"

She sank miserably into a chair. "That night after the party," she said baldly. "She saw you. Remember?"

He flushed a hot red. "The night I – was so – "

"The night you tried to kiss me," Barbara said clearly. "Before Mary died. I was afraid at the time that she had, and now I'm sure – "

"Oh my God!" Geoffrey turned and he, too, stared out of the big window. "Oh my God!"

There was a pause. "Now what?" Barbara asked eventually.

"How do you mean?"

"Do we – go on with our plans? Or change them?"

He turned then, to come and stand beside her. "We go on, of course," he said with sudden decision. "Don't you see? To tell her now that we won't marry will make her believe that we – we feel guilty about it. She must understand that this is a – practical arrangement. If we go ahead, she *will* understand. If we don't, she'll think she was right and that we were having – having an affair before her mother's death, and that it was because she knew that we gave in to her – blackmail."

"She isn't trying to blackmail us, Geoffrey!" Barbara was angry. "That's a horrible suggestion!"

"I know she isn't – now. But if we do change our plans, she might think *we* saw it as that! Don't you see?" He pulled her to her feet, to hold her arms in a tight grasp and stare into her face. "She needs you

132

so much, Barbara! The more upset she seems now, the more I am convinced I'm right!"

She took a deep shuddering breath. Then she nodded miserably. "Yes – " she murmured. "I think I understand what you mean – "

They drove back to the hospital in silence. Barbara felt exhausted, wrung dry of any feeling. There had been a brief moment when she had almost convinced herself that it would be better not to marry Geoffrey, better for Josie. A brief moment when it seemed as though her own happiness was possible, happiness with Daniel. But now she felt trapped, trapped by Josie's anger – for anger it surely must be? – trapped by Geoffrey's conviction that the child needed her as a stepmother.

"Stepmother." The word slid into her consciousness like an evil thing. A word that had, for centuries, carried unpleasant associations. "I'm to be a stepmother – and I'll never have a child of my own – " and in her misery, she hardly knew what distressed her most.

Geoffrey wanted her to eat dinner with him, but she couldn't have faced food at all.

"I'll have some milk later," she said. "Forgive me, but I'm dreadfully tired. I'd rather go back to the hospital now."

And with quick understanding, he said no more, driving her to the hospital door and escorting her to the entrance.

"Try not to worry, Barbara," he said as he left her. "I'm certain I'm right. Once we are married, Josie will come round. She – she'll soon be herself again."

And as she dragged her weary body up the stairs, Barbara told herself he was right. She was going to marry Geoffrey, and be Josie's stepmother, and it was the right thing to do. And that was that. A loveless marriage, perhaps, but one day, a loving relationship with her husband's daughter. And the greater promise of Daniel must be forgotten, put away into the recesses of her mind for good and all.

But as she reached the corridor at the head of the stairs, and saw the thin pencil of light under Daniel's door, she realised it wasn't quite all settled. She owed Daniel an explanation, and her nature wouldn't let her avoid offering that explanation. He had asked her to marry him that afternoon. She had never made a direct answer, and even though that hadn't been her fault, she felt she must tell him why she was to marry Geoffrey, try to explain that she had meant no unkindness to Daniel in the way she had, by implication, refused him.

So, with her head high, she tapped on the panels of his door, and stood waiting for him to answer.

Chapter Thirteen

His gruff "Come in!" made her heart sink for a moment, so that she wanted to turn and run to the security of her own room. But she opened the door quietly, and stood for a second blinking a little in the light.

He was sitting at the desk in the corner of the room, his head burnished to a deep auburn by the pool of light from the lamp beside him. There were books all over the desk, and a pile of writing paper in front of him, and he looked up at her with the vacant gaze of a man who has been pulled away from deep concentration. Then, as he saw her, he dropped the pen he was holding, and smoothed his hair with an oddly awkward gesture.

"Er – Barbara – " He got up, and stood straight, his stocky body silhouetted against the lamplight.

'May I talk to you please, Daniel?" Her voice came with an effort, shaking a little.

"Why – er – yes – yes, of course – "

He swept a pile of books off the only other chair in the room, and Barbara sat down gratefully, trying to hide the way her knees were shaking.

There was a stilted silence for a long moment, then Barbara, summoning all the control she had, said in a low voice, "I'd like to explain – about this afternoon – "

"There isn't anything to explain," he said gruffly,

135

"I – I'm a fool, I suppose. I shouldn't have let you leave the Royal as you did, without – oh well." He grinned lopsidedly. "All those years, when I should have realised, and then to let you go off and fall in love with someone else. Serves me right."

"But you don't understand – " Barbara said desperately. "It isn't like that – "

"Isn't like what?" He looked up sharply from the pipe he had started to fill. "You did say you were engaged, didn't you?"

"Oh, yes, I'm engaged," she said drearily. "But – look, let me start at the beginning, and just hear me out, will you? No interruptions."

He nodded, and sat down himself. Then, with her hands clasped firmly on her lap, and with her eyes fixed on them so that she would not have to look at Daniel's face, she told him.

She told him everything. The hostility between herself and Mary, the way Josie had burst out with her dislike of her mother, the way Barbara herself felt about Josie, and to a lesser extent, Jamie. Geoffrey's behaviour after the party, and the fact that Josie had been a witness to it. With her voice dropped lower, she tried to tell him how she had envied Mary her position and security, how she had suddenly feared her own lonely future, and then of her guilt when Mary had died while the two of them were on such bad terms.

Telling him about Geoffrey's proposal, and what it involved, was even harder. But with her usual honesty, she made no attempt to gloss over the financial benefit to herself, while still trying to make him see why she felt so strongly about Josie's need for her. She finished by telling him of what had happened with Josie that

136

afternoon, and let her voice die away at last into silence.

He made no move, keeping his unlit pipe stuck firmly between his teeth. When at last she raised her eyes to his, she felt, almost like a physical blow, the look of cold anger on his face.

"You don't understand," she said flatly.

"I understand all too well." His voice was harsh. "You – you're marrying a man you don't care for."

"But you must see *why* – " she said almost piteously. It suddenly mattered quite dreadfully that Daniel should not only understand, but agree that she was right – that she had no other course to take than the one she contemplated.

"Why? To make life comfortable for a man who cares so little for you that he'd marry you knowing you don't love him? For a child who probably doesn't need you as much as you think she does?"

"But she does!"

"Look, Barbara. I'm no psychiatrist, and I've never met the girl. But from what you say about her, it's pretty clear to me that she needs more than *your* high-minded sacrifice to help her. She's sick with guilt because her mother died after she said she wanted her to. Do you honestly think you can help that guilt by making the rest of her wild fantasy come true?"

"Wild fantasy?" Barbara said wonderingly.

"For God's sake – " His anger boiled over suddenly. "Use your brains, you idiot! The child says she wishes her own mother was dead, and that you were her mother instead. And then her mother is killed – and you propose to *become* her mother instead! Are you *trying* to make the child feel like a murderer?"

137

"Oh no – no," Barbara whispered, horror in her eyes. "It can't be like that – "

He stood up, and began to pace around the shabby room. "This is impossible, Barbara. I'm no one to influence you. Perhaps you *are* right – I don't know. All I know is that I love you. And while I'd accept your marriage to someone else you cared for, the thought of you getting tied up to someone you don't love and who doesn't love you makes me physically sick. So don't ask me what you should do – "

"I'm not asking you." Barbara was stung. "I'm just trying to tell you why – why I couldn't accept your – accept you. I wanted you to know that it wasn't because – "

She stopped suddenly. What was she going to say? That she *did* care for him? That she would have fallen into his arms if he had only asked her sooner?

"There isn't much point in this," she said bitterly. "It's all a mess."

"Mess is the right word." His anger was still simmering. "But if you want to make a mess of your life, it's your business. I think you're being a damned fool, but that's you, isn't it? You think too much – and you're so busy thinking, you haven't time to have any sense."

"I'm trying to do the right thing," she said dully. "If that's thinking too much – "

"If you spent less time trying to do the right thing, as you put it, and did what you *wanted* to do, perhaps you'd make less misery for yourself – and for other people – "

"It's *you* that's being stupid," she flared. "It's all so easy for you, isn't it? If I did what I wanted, I'd marry

138

you, and that's what you want – " She stopped, aghast at herself.

He stared at her for a brief moment, and then, moving with a speed that almost frightened her, he was beside her, pulling her into his arms with rough urgency, kissing her as she had never been kissed in her life before. She tried to resist, tried to regain her composure, but it was useless. She found herself responding with a passion she never knew she had in her, clinging to him desperately, losing herself in the strange rush of new sensations, new feelings, so that her whole body seemed to melt in a fire of emotion.

"Christ, Barbara," he was muttering, "you *can't* marry this man – you can't – I love you – Barbara – "

But with an almost superhuman effort, she pulled away from him, to lean, breathless and near tears, against the door.

"No – " She pushed him away with both hands. "No – "

He clenched his fists with sudden rage. "Barbara! What's the matter with you? Are you mad? How can you let a man you don't love marry you? How can you consider it? – to have his children – "

She closed her eyes in an effort to stop seeing his face. "It won't be like that – it won't be that sort of marriage – "

It was as though she had flung iced water in his face. "Not that sort of marriage?" he said slowly at last. "Not that sort of marriage? You mean – "

She opened her eyes and looked at him then. "No," she said bitterly. "No children. No – love of that kind at all. Does that make it better?"

"Better?" He was shouting now. "Better? It's worse!

139

He buys you as housekeeper, is that it? Denies you the right to have children of your own, so that you can look after him and *his* blasted children? What are you? A lump of – of earth? You're a woman, Barbara – a real woman. What sort of life are you planning, for God's sake? Sterile – "

"Stop it!" In her pain, in her own state of turmoil, she did something that shocked her – she hit him, pulling her arm back to throw every scrap of her strength into the blow.

He stood there, flaming-faced and with eyes that glittered with fury.

"Get out of here." His voice was choked. "Get out before – " And he pulled the door open, and nearly threw her into the corridor.

She crept to her room like a whipped child. Her body ached and trembled, her head was spinning with words, her face was twisted into lines of pain and misery. She almost collapsed on to her bed, to dissolve into floods of tears, sobbing as though her body would tear apart with her grief. She wept for herself, for Daniel, for the sudden realisation that she had promised to deny herself for always the passion she now knew she had. Daniel's touch, his urgent kisses, had woken her in a way she thought she could never be woken, had opened a door for a brief second – a door that she herself was closing. Because, through her tears, through her misery, she knew she could not go through that door, to the life and promise of Daniel. She had told Geoffrey she would marry him – and that was that. No backing out.

And when the storm of tears had subsided, when she could think again, she knew why she had to marry Geoffrey. It wasn't the security. Indeed, the thought of that now made her want to scream to the world that it didn't matter. It was Josie, Josie and her guilt, if that was what it was. Barbara, confused and desperately unhappy, clung to that thought. She, and only she, could help Josie now. No one else. Even if Daniel was right, and Josie did feel as though she had herself killed her mother, then Barbara, who had heard her say she wanted to be rid of her mother, was the only one who could understand, and help her.

When she fell asleep at last, her conviction had crystallised firmly at last. She *would* marry Geoffrey, come hell or high water.

Chapter Fourteen

The next few weeks were misery for Barbara. She worked through each day dully, with little of the pleasure she was used to finding in her work. It was this that was hardest of all to bear. She had been prepared to find working with Daniel difficult, and though his cool professional attitude towards her hurt, she was able to understand, and even be grateful for the professional relationship that made it possible to work with a man after a stormy emotional passage such as they had had. But work – the work she loved, that had always been her own cure for her personal troubles – that this should let her down, as it were, lose its attraction – that was really painful.

But, with the habit of years, the training that was now so much a part of her, she managed to hide her distress, and carry on apparently as usual. The little hospital filled up for a few weeks, with the early bronchitis attacks, the occasional pneumonia patient, and the routine minor surgery that the local people saved to have dealt with until after the summer rush of visitors to the town was over.

Early in November, she went into Dover to see the consultant at the hospital there, and to have a barium meal to discover whether, in fact, her ulcer,

142

the ulcer that had brought her to Sandleas, was cured.

It was. She found this ironic, as she listened to the consultant telling her his opinion.

"You're quite fit again, Miss Hughes, though I must say you're a bit thinner than you should be. It wouldn't hurt you to put on a few pounds. But apart from that, there's no reason why you should not return to theatre work. I gather you want to go back to London again to work?"

"I did," Barbara said. "But now – I'm getting married, so I shall be staying in Sandleas."

"Congratulations! Though I hope you won't give up work immediately? Good nurses are hard to come by! Unless of course, you decide to start a family right away!" and he had laughed cheerfully, and written "Discharged" at the foot of her case notes.

Sitting on the train on her way back to Sandleas, Barbara squirmed at the memory of his words. A family. Children of her own. How much would she regret throwing away for ever the possibility of having her own babies? Before Daniel had arrived at Sandleas, the thought had never entered her mind. Children were delightful, of course, but she had never really imagined herself as a mother. But since Daniel had come back, she had found herself thinking of children more and more. Children with red hair and stocky square little bodies –

But this was dangerous thinking. She had no right to such thoughts. She was to marry Geoffrey.

"I suppose there's a lot to be said for a peaceful unemotional marriage," she told herself defiantly, watching the green Kentish countryside slide by. "No

143

arguments, no misery." She remembered the friends of her training days who had married, remembered the emotional storms and miseries so many of them had seemed to go through with their new husbands, and comforted herself with the thought that she would escape all that. But it was cold comfort.

December came, bringing with it a flurry of activity in the hospital. Patients who were well enough spent long hours making Christmas decorations for the wards, Matron immured herself in the office with long lists of the food she would have to buy for the patients' and staff's Christmas celebrations, and nurses could be discovered making Christmas presents in the kitchen when they should have been cleaning cupboards or making beds.

Barbara tried to throw herself into these preparations, but it wasn't easy. She would be sorting through last year's decorations, or collecting the new ones that patients had made, when Daniel would come into the ward to see a patient, and she would feel obscurely guilty about what she had been doing. Which was absurd, because in the old days at the Royal he had been as much involved with these tasks as the nursing staff. But now he seemed not to notice that Christmas was in the air, concentrating on work and work only. He never said a word to Barbara that was not to do with purely medical matters.

And then, it was December the nineteenth, and Josie was due home for the holidays. Jamie had arranged to spend Christmas with a friend in Scotland, but Barbara nonetheless promised herself that she would do her best to make Christmas in the big comfortable, yet dreary, Martin house as cheerful as she could. On the day Josie was due home, she took a taxi to the house, loaded with decorations for the tree Geoffrey had promised to order, and with her own gifts for the household.

Josie was already there when Barbara let herself into the house. She could see the pile of luggage beside the front door. She dropped her parcels in the hall, and went up to the yellow room at the top of the stairs to see her niece.

She had already unpacked some of her bags and was sitting on her bed writing a letter when Barbara knocked and put her head round the door.

"Hello, darling!" she said with a forced cheerfulness. "Nice to be home?"

Josie looked up, and then carefully put her letter away before answering.

"Hello, Auntie Barbara. Yes thank you." But there was no warmth in her voice, no flicker of real pleasure.

Barbara wanted desperately to sit beside Josie, to put her arms round her, to try to break down some of this icy reserve, but she knew instinctively that this would be wrong. It was no use to try and rush Josie – she must be allowed to thaw in her own good time.

"And I'm sure she will," Barbara told herself optimistically, later that evening, when she and Josie and Geoffrey sat down together for dinner.

It wasn't an easy meal. Barbara did her best to make conversation, but Josie blocked her every attempt and Geoffrey, too, seemed abstracted. As the meal progressed, Barbara would catch him looking at her with an unusual intensity, as though he were trying to reach a decision, and when he caught her eye, he would drop his own gaze in a somehow childish sort of confusion.

145

After dinner, Josie went up to her room. "I've got some letters to write," she said sullenly, when Geoffrey asked her what she was doing. And when Barbara tried to speak, to persuade Josie to spend the evening with them in the drawing-room, he shook his head at her, and let Josie go up to shut herself in her room, alone.

"She's better alone, if she wants to be," he said, as he followed Barbara into the drawing-room, and watched her start to pour the coffee. "And I want to talk to you, my dear. I seem to have seen so little of you lately – "

"I've been rather busy," Barbara said defensively. "Christmas preparations for the hospital and all that – "

But she knew she lied. She had been avoiding Geoffrey, making excuses not to go to the house, finding reasons for not going out to dinner with him in the town's restaurants, on the occasions he had asked her to. It wasn't that she didn't want to see him so much as that she wanted time to herself, to get used to the idea of marrying him, for the fact that she was engaged to this man still seemed strange. And behind her reasoning, she had instinctively been holding on to her independence for as long as she could, because the time when she would no longer be her own mistress, but the wife of Geoffrey Martin, Solicitor, was coming very near. But she hardly realised this herself.

"Drink?" He brought her a liqueur, and settled into his chair with his own usual glass of brandy. They sat silently for a while, Barbara sipping her coffee, Geoffrey staring abstractedly into the fire.

Barbara was just beginning to wonder if he did in fact want to talk about anything special, when he pulled himself to his feet, and went out into the hall to bring in his briefcase.

He took a sheaf of papers out of it, and put them on the coffee table in front of Barbara.

"These are the papers to do with the marriage settlement, and so on," he said awkwardly. "If you could sign them, I'll get Mrs. Lester to come in and witness your signature."

Barbara looked at the official typed documents with distaste. "Must I?" she asked diffidently. "This all seems so mercenary, somehow. I'd really rather not – "

He came and stood close beside her, to look down on to her bent head. "It is necessary, my dear," he said, his voice oddly thick. "We did say this was to be a business arrangement – "

She pulled away from him, to get up from her seat and turn to gaze into the fire. "I know – " she said in a low voice. "But it's all – so – "

She felt him behind her, felt his breath on her bent neck.

"You dislike the idea of a business-like marriage?" There was an odd urgency in the question.

She bit her lip. "I suppose I do, really," she said, trying to understand her own feelings, wanting to explain that the thought of signatures on official documents made her embarrassed.

"Thank God," he said softly, and almost before she realised it, he had pulled her round, to hold her firmly in his arms, pinning her against him with sudden strength. "I don't want that sort of marriage either, my darling," he said, his voice low, yet exultant. "I must have been mad to try and persuade myself that I did. I've been trying to tell myself that you wanted it this way, that you didn't care for me at all, but now – "

She was almost dumb with the shock. Not wanting to

sign documents had nothing to do with her feelings for Geoffrey. She knew that – but he didn't.

"He couldn't think I meant I cared for him," she thought in sudden wild panic, and tried to pull away from him. But he was too strong for her. His head was down, his lips hot on hers, his whole body straining against hers in a way that made her want to scream with fear.

"No – no," she managed to get her head away, struggling to escape from his grasp. "No – "

And then, to her sick horror, she saw Josie. She was standing very still and erect, her eyes blazing by the door to the hall, her face so altered with anger that she looked old.

Geoffrey, suddenly aware of Barbara's rigid body, looked over his shoulder. He dropped his arms from Barbara, and turned to look at his daughter.

"Josie – " He passed his hand over his hair. "Josie – "

"You make me *sick*!"

Her voice was low, but the intensity of loathing in it made it beat on Barbara's ears like a scream.

"You – you're my *father*!"

And then, almost to her surprise, Barbara heard her own voice, cool and clear.

"Josie, come here." Josie ignored her, staring only at Geoffrey.

"Josie! Do as you are told and come here." The unexpected authority in her aunt's voice made Josie turn to look at her, and almost as though against her will, she came and stood in front of them both.

Barbara thrust her hands into the pockets of her suit jacket, more to hide their trembling than anything else.

As she stood looking at the tight, angry face, it was as though everything whirled and then clicked into place. At the back of her mind she could hear Daniel's voice saying "wild fantasy". She could see herself as she had been these past weeks, blinded by her own stubbornness, by her fears for Josie. And she knew, really knew at last, what she should do.

Then she spoke.

"Josie," she said gently, "you're very young, and you have had a good deal to suffer and understand this past few months. But young as you are, I think you are able to understand what I am going to say, and I expect you to listen with an attempt at intelligence. We have tried to treat you with kid gloves, but the time for that is past. You are now going to listen to me, and listen with calmness and good sense. Right?"

Josie looked back at her for a moment. Then she said, "Will you tell me what I want to know – not just what you think I should know?"

"I shall try to," Barbara said with a forced calmness.

"All right." And Josie sat down on the pouffe by the fire.

"When I first came to live here, last spring, you were finding life difficult with your mother." It was a statement, not a question. There was a fleeting look of pain on Josie's face, but Barbara hurried on.

"And then I arrived, an outsider, and yet an outsider you knew, and someone who had a job you thought was a glamorous one. And like so many girls of your age, you got a – a crush on me. Am I right?"

Josie flushed scarlet. "I – I – "

"Don't try to answer if you find it difficult. But I

149

think you understand me. Then, one evening, you were particularly upset with your mother because of something she had said about me, and you told me that you wanted your mother to go away – that you wished I were your mother instead."

Josie had dropped her head so that her fine hair flopped forward to hide her face. Barbara, acutely aware of Geoffrey standing rigid and silent beside her, took a deep breath and went on.

"And then your mother and I – argued. And we parted on bad terms. And you were angry with both of us. Very angry. You felt I had run out on you when you wanted me to stay, and you hated your mother as well for letting it happen. And then – "

Barbara's voice faltered, then strengthened. "And then there was the accident. And because you loved your mother, even though you had been angry with her, you felt that her death had been your fault."

Josie, her head still bent, said nothing, but her narrow shoulders moved a little.

Barbara fell on her knees beside the child, to look up into the face hidden in the floppy hair. "Darling Josie, you have no need to feel like that – really you haven't! What happened to your mother would have happened whatever you had felt or thought. *You had nothing to do with it!* You *must* understand that. Nothing at all."

And at last Josie was crying, tears falling unheeded down her face as she rocked her small body to and fro in an ecstasy of tears, while Barbara, her heart light with relief of seeing the unchildish reserve broken at last, held her close, letting the tears fall as they would, making no attempt to stop them.

Gradually, the sobs lessened. Then Josie said, her

voice choked and almost too quiet to be heard. "But you're going to marry Daddy – *you* wanted Mummy to die too – "

"Oh Josie, Josie – I didn't!" Barbara put a hand under Josie's chin, forcing her to raise her head and look at her. "But when your father asked me to marry him, he told me that it was because he wanted me to look after you – to take your mother's place. I was foolish enough to think I could, darling, but I think I know now that I couldn't possibly – "

Josie, still breathing the uneven dragging gulps of her tears looked over Barbara's shoulder at Geoffrey, still standing unmoving by the fire.

"But he loves you!" she cried, her voice full of accusation. "I've seen you – that party – and now – "

"Yes, Josie, I do." Geoffrey's harsh voice was a shock, almost. "Is that so dreadful? You love Barbara too, don't you?"

"Auntie Bar is my *aunt*," Josie said flatly.

Barbara got to her feet, wearily. "Yes, Jo," she said gently. "I'm your aunt. And I hope you will always love me as an aunt. But you need never try to think of me as a replacement for your mother, because I'm not going to try to be one." And she looked directly at Geoffrey, trying to show her compassion for his distress in her face.

He looked back at her, and then with a voice so full of pain that Barbara could have wept, he said, "You won't?"

"No Geoffrey." She was gentle. "I said I would marry you because of Josie. And for no other reason. But that's no basis for a marriage. Even if Josie really wanted me as a stepmother, it wouldn't work. I need – so much more.

To try to be happy with you would be impossible – and unfair to you. I can't do it. I'm sorry."

He said nothing, staring at her, looking at her face as though he would never see it again, as though he wanted to imprint every line of it on his memory.

Barbara looked again at Josie. "I'm going away, Jo. A long way away. One day I'll see you again, but not for a long time – not until you've grown up, probably. You will have to make yourself happy, darling. No one can do that for you. I was arrogant enough to think I could, but I know I can't."

There was no more to say. It had all been said, even if not in so many words. For Barbara, looking at Geoffrey's ravaged face, her own stupidity in ever thinking she could marry him made her hate herself. She had wanted to help these two, wanted to make their lives happy even at the expense of her own happiness.

But even if she *had* married him on their original terms this time would have come, she knew. He would have had to face the fact that she could never love him, as he wanted her to, accept the loneliness that had always been a part of his marriage, and would now continue to be a part of his life alone.

Slowly, Barbara walked to the door. She looked back for a moment at Josie sitting still on her pouffe, staring up at her father, at Geoffrey, straight and alone in his unhappiness. And then she went.

The last thing she saw of the house was the pile of parcels in gay Christmas paper that she had dropped on the chair in the hall. Then she closed the door, and walked back through the raw December darkness to the hospital.

It was as though she were another person. The

152

Barbara she had always been, the cool composed elegant woman she knew as herself seemed to be far away. Now, she was someone else, someone who had been a fool, and knew it, someone who knew now what she wanted, and was going to get it.

The main hall of the hospital was dim and quiet, the shape of the Christmas tree that was waiting to be trimmed looming darkly in one corner. Quietly she climbed the uneven old staircase, listening with one ear to the night-time sounds of the hospital around her. One of the children in the babies' ward was crying, the sleepy cry of a child too tired and cross to let himself sleep. Someone was rattling dishes in the kitchen, preparing the night nurses' midnight meal, and from the corridor above she could hear the sound of bathwater running in Matron's bathroom.

At the top of the stairs she stopped for a moment, looking at the narrow pencil of light under Daniel's door. And then, her head high, she went across the polished floor, and pushed open the door.

He was sitting at the desk in the corner, his hair ruffled and shining redly in the lamplight. As the door opened, he lifted his head to look at her, his face blank and stupefied.

She stood there for a long moment, her smooth dark head thrown up, her slender body rigid. And then she said softly, "Daniel."

He stared at her for a long moment, and then stood up, his face shadowed as his body blocked out the light.

She took a deep breath. "Daniel," she said again, "I love you. Will you marry me?"

153

And she closed the door behind her, plunging the corridor outside back into its dim quiet.

And in the babies' ward, the crying child gulped once more, and fell into the sudden sleep of the very young.